"That was

She waited

with Kade, but after a few silent beats passed, she decided to nudge further, refusing to dissect why it mattered. "You lost someone."

Another minuscule movement. A slight nod. "Sergeant Nylan. Shayla's fiancé."

Her chin shot up. "Oh. Amelia's father." She'd wondered about him, but had never asked. It wasn't any of her business, and if her friend had wanted to talk, she'd listen. If not, that was fine, too.

What wasn't fine, was the dark expression on the handsome doctor's face as he continued to stare at the photo, when just a few minutes ago, he could've lit the night. Even though she didn't want to pester, she just couldn't let him dwell in that dark place. "If it brings back a bad memory, why leave it up?"

For some reason, the thought of him being transported back to that moment over and over, bothered her more than it should. Which made no sense. Heck, they weren't even technically friends. And yet, it did bother her, laying like a piece of lead in her stomach.

"I leave it up there to remind me I'm not infallible. That I can't save everyone. That I'm…"

"Human," she whispered, throat suddenly too tight to breath.

"Yeah."

Once again, her mind tried to comprehend the man. A doctor. Who cared about people. She knew that was technically what doctors were supposed to do, but in her experience, it tipped the other way. Big time. In her experience, the title often meant more than the oath taken.

What they're saying...

About Wyne and Dine:

"The Citizen Soldier series has a fantastic new addition with Wyne and Chocolate. The book had a great start. I found myself laughing out loud right away - and that set the tone for a light-hearted, funny, and romantic read. I've read a LOT of romance books, and Wyne and Chocolate has one of the best first kisses that I have read."

—Reviewer- Romancereader

About Her Uniform Cowboy:

"Ms. Michaels pens a tale with pure heart and true grit! This story will hit so many readers close to home there is not one part of the plot that will feel foreign. No super models here, just true, down to earth servicemen and woman getting back to their place in the world. The characters and plot have a wonderful arc and the laughter, tears and emotional ride readers get to take on this journey will not disappoint."

—InD'tale Magazine, Crowned Heart of Excellence 4.5 Stars
--Voted BEST COWBOY in a Book/Reader's Choice-LRC
--Finalist BTS eMagazine Red Carpet Book Award/Reader's Choice-Best Romance & Best Book 2014

About Her Forever Cowboy:

"Ms. Michaels has done it again! Book four in this series is another great success. The author knows how to lure her readers in by telling them a wonderful story that's wrapped around characters we get to know and love as if they're real people. This book was no exception. I highly recommend this book and this author!"

—Night Owl Reviews, *Reviewer Top Pick*
--July Read of the Month--SSYL
--Nominee BTS Magazine Red Carpet Book Award/Reader's Choice-Romance 2014

Dear Reader,

Thank you for purchasing Her Healing Cowboy. This is the fifth book in my Harland County Series. *Unruly cowboys and the women who tame them...*

This book is about Kade's buddy, Jace Turner, a doctor and Captain in the Texas National Guard. With his lifelong goal of joining Doctors without Borders on the horizon when his contract is up in the Guard, and his free time spent helping his mother and sister on the family ranch, Jace is not looking for love.

Holly Phillips just received a coveted promotion at a Colorado ski resort, but takes a leave-of-absence to take over her uncle's Harland County ice cream shop while he recovers from surgery. Growing up with an aversion to doctors, she's confused by her attraction to her uncle's general practitioner. She's only in town temporarily, so giving into the attraction wouldn't be smart. Too bad her heart has other ideas.

This is another hot, heartfelt, sexy read in this series involving some series regulars, and introducing a few new ones.

Thanks for reading,

~Donna
www.donnamichaelsauthor.com

Also by Donna Michaels

~Novels~

Wyne and Chocolate (Citizen Soldier Series-Book Two)

Wyne and Dine (Citizen Soldier Series-Book One)

Captive Hero (Time-shift Heroes Series-Book One)

The Spy Who Fanged Me

Her Fated Cowboy (Harland County Series-Book One)

Her Unbridled Cowboy (Harland County Series-Book Two)

Her Uniform Cowboy (Harland County Series-Book Three)

Her Forever Cowboy (Harland County Series-Book Four)

She Does Know Jack

Royally Unleashed

~Novellas~

Harland County Christmas (Novella/Brock and Jen)

Cowboy-Fiancé (formerly Cowboy-Sexy)

Thanks for Giving

Ten Things I'd Do for a Cowboy

Vampire Kristmas

~Short Stories~

The Hunted

Negative Image

The Truth About Daydreams

Holiday Spirit

~Do-Over Series~

Valentine's Day Do-Over

Valentine's Day Do-Over Part II: The Siblings

UPCOMING RELEASES:

Cowboy Payback (Cowboy-Fiancé Sequel)

~Time-shift Heroes Series~

Future Hero—Book Two

~Harland County Series~

Her Volunteer Cowboy (Book 6/Tanner)

~Citizen Soldier Novels~

Wyne and Song (Book 3/Ethan)

Her Healing Cowboy

A Harland County Novel
Book 5: Jace

By
NY Times & USA Today Bestselling Author
Donna Michaels

HER HEALING COWBOY

A Harland County Series Novel//Book 5: Jace

ISBN-13: 978-1512344851
ISBN-10: 1512344850

Print edition May 2015

Dedication

To my readers for their wonderful support. To my family, the HOODS, and the Minion Division—my wonderful street team.♥

Chapter One

Hot and bothered, and not in a good way, Holly Phillips carried a tray of sundaes she made to her friends waiting for her at a table outside The Creamery, her uncle's ice cream shop. With the temperature still in the eighties, she weaved around customers enjoying the final weekend in September, while she secretly longed for the cooler temperatures at her home in Denver.

A life-long snow bunny, she'd been stuck in south Texas for two months longer than planned. Harland County and its folks were nice, but lacked one very important thing.

Snow.

Her skis and snowboard would get about as much action as she was in the little gulf coast town. Not that there weren't plenty of hot prospects for the latter, and equally hot propositions from some sexy cowboys. But, she wasn't staying any longer than her uncle needed her to run his business, so there was no reason to get involved, or at the very least, naked, with anyone.

Suppressing a sigh, she set the tray on the table and sat with her two new friends. The Ryan sisters. "I come bearing gifts."

Dressed in tan capris and turquoise top, Shayla Ryan, soon-to-be Shayla Dalton, reached for the CMP with extra whipped cream, her mega karat diamond glinting in the sun. "You are a goddess among women."

"And you are going to blind someone with your ring, sis." Caitlin Ryan squinted against the glare, looking cool and cute in denim shorts and pink tank top. "Kevin sure doesn't pull any punches. He's already spoiling Amelia. I can only imagine what he has in store for the new baby."

The beautiful mother smiled, lovingly touching the small swell of her tummy. "He's a great daddy to my daughter, and this baby of ours is going to be just as lucky."

Having witnessed the handsome cowboy swoop in and rescue Shayla from her abusive father a few weeks back, fierce love and devotion shining in his eyes, Holly knew her friend had found a true gem.

At least *he* wouldn't cheat if his girlfriend worked long hours.

"To Kevin." She held up a spoonful of ice cream, and after the others echoed her toast, they dug into their chocolate, marshmallow, and peanut sundaes.

Almost four months ago, Holly had arrived in Harland County to run The Creamery while her Uncle Arthur had his hip replaced. The timing couldn't have been worse. She'd just nailed the promotion she'd worked her ass off to get—losing her boyfriend and best friend in the process when the traitors went from keeping each other company in her absence to sleeping together. Her new position as Assistant Marketing Director at a very popular Ski Resort was now more coveted than ever. It cost her a lot, and she was damn sure going to enjoy it.

She hoped.

"When does your uncle go back to the doctor?" Caitlin asked, hooking a strand of light brown hair behind her ear before eating another spoonful.

"This Wednesday."

Finally.

Her mother's only living relative, and Holly's godfather, was supposed to be out no more than twelve weeks in the first stage of his recovery. His short-term recovery. The part where he learned to walk with no aid and no major pain medications. Her mom came down with her and moved in with her uncle to physically take care of him while Holly took care of his ice cream business. Once he made headway into his long-term recovery and could go back to work, she was supposed to be able to go back to her own job. And to her younger brother Zach, whom she shared an apartment with near the university he attended.

Short-term was now going on sixteen weeks. She was four weeks past her leave-of-absence, grateful the ski resort had granted her a six week extension. But that was rapidly running out, like her patience.

The only bright spot was the cute little gulf cottage within walking distance to the shop. With its light blue walls and white cabinetry and woodwork, the quaint house actually felt like a home. More so than her state-of-the-art, up-to-date condo she rented in Colorado.

It was stark. Like her love life.

"Is it with Jace?" Shayla stared at her, slight smile curving her lips.

It took Holly a moment to realize her friend was asking about her uncle's doctor appointment.

"No. Not him."

Thank God. Try as she might, Holly couldn't stop the flash of heat from spreading through her body. Just the mere mention of the gorgeous doctor's name sent her temperature soaring, and she was already hot.

Her gaze strayed to the handsome, shirtless man playing volleyball in the sand several yards away. She knew him. He was one of her uncle's doctors. They'd met several times at the hospital and in his office. The general practitioner was always cool and professional, never out of line. A perfect gentleman. And so sexy her ovaries hurt.

Doctor Jace Turner was too damn potent and a boatload of trouble to her peace of mind. One she did her best to avoid.

She swiped a hand across her damp forehead and shifted on the bench. “Uncle Arthur is seeing his orthopedic surgeon, not Jace…Doctor Turner,” she corrected. “He’s his general practitioner. But I think my uncle has a follow up with him next week.”

Even though her mom was taking care of her uncle and living on the man’s ranch, Gloria Phillips did not drive. So, it was up to Holly to cart everyone around. With luck, after this checkup, only for a few more days.

Then, hopefully, she would be free to head back home to Colorado. And her real job.

If it still existed.

“Fingers are crossed all goes well,” her friend said, holding up her hand and crossing her fingers.

She was lucky to have the Ryan sisters to keep her sane.

Three months ago, they’d met under interesting circumstances at this very table. Shayla had been sitting with two men, and Holly had realized something was off when she heard raised voices and saw the big guy grabbing Shayla’s arm. Without hesitation and under the pretense of inquiring if the ice cream was satisfactory, she’d stepped from behind the counter to investigate. The men had immediately said yes, but she’d noted the bruising on the woman’s arm and the fear in her eyes. Not fear for herself; no, it had been a fear for those around her getting hurt. Holly had gone back inside and called the police, keeping her eye on Shayla while waiting for the sheriff.

His deputy had arrived first. Holly smiled at the memory of the dark-eyed, brown-haired, Jordan McCall—now Sheriff McCall—face-slamming the big guy into the table. Three times. It had warmed her heart, almost as much as Shayla's concern for others. The pretty redhead's worry for complete strangers was the reason Holly had taken another chance at friendship, after having been burnt so bad.

And she'd gotten a twofer out of the deal. The woman's younger sister turned out just as sweet and loyal.

"Hopefully, the doctor will give your uncle the green light to go back to work." Caitlin smiled.

The twenty-three-year-old was in her sophomore year at college, having started late because of her abusive dad, the sickly man that had been harassing Shayla. But he was now behind bars, and the girls no longer had to run.

Having grown up with a neglectful father who left her mother with two young children after she'd worked two jobs to put him through medical school, Holly could relate a little with the tough childhood her new friends had endured. At least she'd had the support of a loving mother. Still, judging by their relaxed posture and cheerful expressions, the sisters were moving on.

"Yeah, maybe this will be the week, although, we don't want to see you go," Shayla quickly added, setting her spoon down, her sundae demolished. "I was hoping you'd be at my wedding."

Holly swallowed the last of her ice cream and nodded. "I wouldn't miss it. I'll be here, even if I have to drive back down."

A big smile brightened the bride-to-be's expression. "That's wonderful to hear. It wouldn't be the same without you." The woman reached across the table to squeeze her hand before releasing her to sit back. "Hell, if it wasn't for you, I might not even be having one." Tears filled her pretty blue eyes and spilled down her cheek. "Stupid hormones," she muttered, swiping the wetness from her face. "I can't seem to stop the waterworks. I even cry at commercials, now."

She nodded. "Those humane society ones get me all the time."

"Not just those. I cry at potato chip commercials. Department store commercials. Beer commercials. It's damned tiring."

Caitlin's chuckle echoed hers and Shayla's.

"Speaking of weddings, you haven't told me much about the wedding you attended in Pennsylvania. You've been back three days." She sat back and eyed the girls closely. "How did it go?"

Color flooded Caitlin's cheeks. "It was great."

"Yeah." Shayla nodded, dreamy look crossing her face. "Brandi was beautiful and glowing in a white gown with just the right amount of embroidery and lace, and Kade…wow."

"He looked so handsome in a tux," Caitlin said.

"Almost as good as my Kevin.

Brandi was Shayla's boss, and soon-to-be kin having just married Kevin's cousin. Those Dalton men were gorgeous and generous, always tipping, no matter how small the order. Her friend was marrying into a nice family, and she was so happy for her.

"Well, the two of you are going to look amazing. I can't wait," she said, before transferring her gaze to the younger sister who had gone quiet. "And I also can't wait to hear why you blushed when you said you had a great time at the wedding."

"What?" Caitlin blinked. "I didn't blush. It's just hot out here."

Shayla snorted. "Nice try, sis, but I saw you openly flirting with Brandi's youngest brother, Keiffer. The two of you were looking mighty cozy."

Color rose in Caitlin's face, again.

"Ah, judging by that shade of crimson, I'd say you two did more than flirt."

The young woman shrugged. "He made me forget to be miserable. It was nice to feel wanted."

Envy pierced Holly heart, followed by guilt. Shame on her. Caitlin deserved to be happy. The pretty college student's ex was in the air force and had broken off their relationship before he headed to his duty station overseas.

"Good for you," she said with a nod. "I'm glad to hear you had fun."

"Doc Turner looked like he was having fun, too," Shayla remarked. "Those Pennsylvania girls were all over him at the reception."

Without her permission, her gaze drifted back to the hot guy in the sand, muscles rippling as he jumped up and spiked a ball.

Women in the county fawned over him, and she attributed the appeal to his oozing testosterone, lean muscles, ready smile…and profession. She was immune, although her body disagreed. She ignored her body. The man was dangerous with a capital D, and she was not in the market for danger. Or a doctor. Thanks to her father, and her ex, they were low on her list of guys she wanted to date. So low in fact, they weren't even on the list.

Like the others playing volleyball, he wore dark, wraparound sunglasses, but she knew his eyes were as blue as the sky, and just as brilliant, keen, never missed a thing.

Sun glistened off the sweat clinging to a mouthwatering, muscled torso sprinkled with a smattering of dark hair. No man had the right to look that good.

Her chest tightened for some unknown reason.

She probably should've made smaller sundaes.

"True." Caitlin nodded, scraping the last of her ice cream from the cup with her spoon. "Jace does tend to have that affect on women. He's really such a nice guy."

Shayla leveled her sister with a direct stare. "You should know. You've been out with him a few times."

Holly attributed the sudden knotting in her stomach to the smaller sundae scenario and refocused on the conversation.

"Just as friends. He's not interested in me that way." The brown-haired beauty glanced at her and smiled. "Now, *Holly*, that's another story."

She scoffed. "What are you talking about? He's not interested in me, other than what flavor I scoop into his dish."

Although, there were times when she admittedly wouldn't mind indulging in some private taste-testing with the gorgeous man, despite the fact his occupation left a sour taste in her mouth. But, those were times when she was weak and his sexiness fogged the sense from her damn brain, allowing need and lust to take over.

Stupid body.

"I think he likes *all* your flavors, Hol."

She snorted. "You're so full of it, Shayla."

"No, it's true," Caitlin insisted. "His gaze lingers on you when you're not looking. Kind of like how yours is lingering on him right now."

"What?" She blinked, transferring her attention off the ripped doctor and back to her grinning friends. "I-I was just trying to see who he was playing volleyball with, that's all."

"Right." Shayla smirked.

Caitlin glanced around her sister to the beach, then fanned herself. "What a view. He's playing with Tanner, Jesse, and a few of their Guard buddies. Wow…that's a lot of muscle."

"Indeed," she agreed, her gaze straying back to the hot doc.

"Well, I hate to pull you from your viewing pleasure, sis, but we've got to go pick Amelia up from the McCalls'," Shayla said, rising to her feet. "Thanks for the dessert, Holly. It was kid approved." The pregnant woman laughed, tapping her barely swelled belly.

She chuckled as she stood and gathered their empty containers onto the tray. "Anytime. It was nice to have someone to take my break with, but I'd better get back, too. Hate to leave Donny unattended for too long."

Shayla nodded while Caitlin smiled.

"Thanks for giving him a job. How's he working out?"

Holly knew the two carpooled to college together, and even though she'd been forewarned about the young man's knack for disaster, she'd hired him part time anyway. "Not bad. He's had a few missteps, but he's coming along."

Too bad the same couldn't be said for the five gallons of vanilla bean melting in the dumpster out back. She was certain Donny no longer confused an almost shut freezer with a completely shut one.

"You're a patient woman," Shayla said with a shake of her head. "But I do feel better knowing he's an ice cream scooper and no longer a Harland County deputy."

She chuckled. "Yeah, I just can't even fathom how that came to be."

"His dad," Caitlin replied, adjusting the strap on her denim and lace, cross-body purse as she stood next to her sister. "But, he says his parents are coming around to his new career choice."

"That's great to hear."

"Yes." Shayla nodded. "He's a wickedly gifted artist."

Dumping their trash in the nearby garbage can, Holly heartily agreed. "I know. I commissioned a seascape from him for the shop," she said, turning to face her friends, empty tray in hand.

Having thumbed through Donny's sketchpad a few weeks back, she'd been stunned by the bumbling kid's talent and had hired him on the spot. He'd needed money while he was in college, and she wanted to make sure he stayed in college to hone his craft, and major in what he wanted to major in. Offering him a part time job and commissioning a landscape set right with her. She liked to help people who deserved a chance, and Donny certainly fell into that category. The young man was pursuing his dream, studying for a degree he chose. Unlike Holly, who earned a degree in a profession that wasn't her first choice.

"I can't wait to see it." Caitlin beamed.

She nodded. "Me, too."

"Same here, but I'd also like to see my little girl, so we'd better get a move on before Mrs. McCall decides it's a good idea to propose keeping Amelia for another night."

Mrs. McCall was the mother of two very handsome sons. Cole was the down-to-earth CEO of a billion dollar Software Company married to the new local sheriff, and Connor was a big, Marlboro man of a cowboy whose dimples made her customers giddy and jealous because he was married to the sheriff's gorgeous sister. Once a week, Mrs. McCall and Mrs. Masters, the mother of their wives, stopped by The Creamery for strawberry sundaes. The pretty, older women were about the same age as her mother, although, life hadn't been as kind to her mom, and it showed.

Holly shook off the sad thought and smiled at her friend. "She's just getting in some practice before her first grandbaby arrives." She walked with the sisters toward the parking lot, grabbing empty trays off the rack above a garbage can along the way.

"I know." Shayla nodded. "But Kerri is due two weeks before me, in the middle of March, so there's lots of time left to spoil my daughter."

"Oh, I somehow don't think that's going to stop once you and Kerri have your babies," she said, having observed both Mrs. McCall and Mrs. Masters with her friend's sweet little three year old during some of those regular visits.

Shayla smiled. "I agree, but Caitlin and I want to see the latest princess movie, and it's always best to have a child with you for cover."

Laughing, Holly bid her friends good-bye before turning back to clean off the rest of the empty outdoor tables. Try as she might, she couldn't stop her gaze from wandering to the men playing volleyball on the beach several yards away. The more they gave to the game, the more she was drawn in, her fingers itching to capture their zest on camera. But, she wasn't there to take pictures; she was there to serve ice cream. Besides, all she had was her phone. Her state of the art camera sat safe and sound at her uncle's ranch waiting for her to have some time off. She couldn't wear it around her neck while dishing out banana splits, or take the chance someone would walk off with her prized possession. She'd scrimped and saved for two years to purchase the beauty.

She studied the beach and the cowboy guardsmen, muscles gleaming in the sun…

Screw it.

Holly set the trays on a table, fished out her cell, and began clicking away, wishing her smart phone had better zoom to capture the trickle of sweat curving down the beautiful sinew of the doctor's back. Just as she was finishing up the last few shots, he stiffened and turned around, his gaze zeroing in on her…and the phone in her hand.

Busted.

Heat rushed to her face, and she sensed his wry amusement when he lifted his hand and waved. Shoot. He probably thought she'd been taking pictures of him.

Okay, she *had*, but not like it seemed. She'd captured the ripple of muscle. Trickle of sweat. Concentration in the brow. The tattoo on the inside of Tanner's left bicep. The doctor's tanned hand as he spiked the ball. His broad shoulders, and ridges in his chest. The sprinkling of hair criss-crossing down washboard abs in an enticing happy trail to the top of navy board shorts…

Ah, crap. She'd been taking pictures of him.

Now, all six of the nearly naked men were grinning and waving at her.

And heading her way.

Double crap.

Heart thudding hard in her chest, she shoved the phone back in the pocket of her shorts, grabbed the trays, and rushed inside the shop. With luck, she'd be elbows deep in water, washing off the trays in her hand by the time the men arrived.

"Hey, Hol, how about six of your smoothie specials?" Tanner's playful tone hit her ears a minute later.

Relief washed through her, relaxing muscles faster than the sigh that burst a batch of bubbles in the sink in front of her. She could deal with Tanner. Earlier that summer, she'd bonded with the volunteer fireman/ranch hand/guardsman over the fact they shared a daredevil gene when they'd met windsurfing on a stormy Sunday.

"Me and the guys kind of worked up a sweat."

"I know," she muttered, wiping her hands, wishing she could wipe away the blush heating her face. "Six Mango Pineapple Beach Blasts coming right up."

"Thanks. We'll be at the shaded table in the corner," he said, before she had the chance to even turn around and ring up the sale, or beg him to wait.

She glanced sideways at Donny. He was in the middle of a large order for a family of five. *Dang*. No hope of asking him to deliver the smoothies.

With another sigh on her lips, she filled the blender with fresh pineapples, mangos, and mango sorbet, blended until smooth, then repeated until she filled six large cups. She dumped the remaining drink into another cup for herself for later. There was no escaping her penance. Best to go take her medicine from the doc.

Smile tugging her lips, she loaded the smoothies onto a tray and set out to do the walk of shame to where the men sat talking and laughing, having donned shirts, but ditched the sunglasses.

As she reached their table, she decided that was a good thing. It would've been way too distracting to have that much prime muscle up close. She had the photos to prove it.

Maybe only the doctor had noticed her taking pictures.

"Ah, here she is, Ms. Shutter-bug," Tanner joked.

So much for wishful thinking.

She should've known the shrewd, volunteer firefighter would've noticed her taking photos. Tanner had been her tour guide and outdoor companion the whole summer, often teasing her about the amount of photos she took. Still, she enjoyed her outings with the smart, witty man who treated her like a sister. It was a refreshing change from the guys hitting on her ever since her boots had hit Harland County soil.

One of the cowboys winked. "Did you get all the shots you needed? Because I'd be glad to pose for you any day, sweetheart."

"Yeah, me, too." The one Caitlin had called Jesse smiled.

"Count me in."

Switching gears, she smiled as she set the tray on the table and watched as six eager hands each grabbed a cup. "Thanks, guys, but I think I got all the shots I needed."

"Are you sure?" Another asked, leaning forward. "Because you didn't even see my good side."

Tanner snickered. "You don't have a good side, Harper."

"Yes he does," Jesse kidded. "He's sitting on it."

Laughter spread around the table, tugging another smile from her lips. The guys had an easy comradery that confirmed Caitlin's earlier observation that the men were all in the National Guard together.

"Okay. Let's give Ms. Phillps a break. I'm sure she has better things to do than put up with you clowns," the doctor finally spoke up, warm blue eyes holding her attention while his deep tone did crazy things to her pulse. "There are plenty of other men still on the beach, and we're keeping her from photographing them."

"Good one, Captain," Harper said, high-fiving the guy next to him.

But Jace Turner didn't feel like celebrating as he watched the beautiful woman with the most incredible green eyes clam up, swivel around, and stomp away. Something inside his chest knotted and squeezed tight. He hadn't meant to hurt her feelings. He'd mistakenly thought she'd be open to more teasing.

Apparently, not.

Holly Phillips was the niece of one of his patients, and they rarely spoke outside of a professional setting, but that didn't stop him from admiring her beauty, strength, and compassion. Because, oh yeah, she definitely had all three.

Her hair was a mass of black silk that barely touched her shoulders and swung about her delicate face in angles that should've looked unkempt, but instead, gave her a wild, exotic air that kick-started his pulse and tempted his fingers to touch. With a bottom lip a little fuller than the top, her mouth was too wide for her heart-shaped face, but wreaked havoc in his dreams, making him want to nibble and taste. Then there were her gorgeous eyes, stunning, mesmerizing, in a light shade of green as clear as a Bermuda shore and rimmed by thick, dark lashes.

"Way to chase the hot girl away, Doc," Harper teased.

Holly was indeed hot, but way too curvy and lush to be called a girl. She was all woman with the quintessential hourglass figure, despite her height at around five-foot-eight-inches tall. But he declined to correct the guy, choosing to drink his smoothie instead.

"None of you stand a chance with her anyway," Tanner said. "She has way too much taste."

"Then why did she go out with you?" Jesse asked, between slurps.

Jace's heart lurched unexpectedly. He hadn't had movement like that in his chest over a woman in a long time. Not since high school when his hormones had run rampant.

"You're seeing Holly?" The question was out before he could stop it, and he was damned if he knew why. She wasn't his type. Too sour and closed up. At least, toward him. He tended to go for warm and friendly. So he didn't understand his fixation with Holly Phillips. Ever since she stepped into his office with her uncle four months ago, he'd felt a jolt to his solar plexus.

A dark brow rose. "Oh, it's Holly now, is it?" The damn guy snickered. "Just a minute ago it was *Ms.* Phillips."

"Cut the crap and answer the question, Tanner." He ignored the other gazes now trained on him as the guys apparently found his conversation more interesting than their drinks.

"Yes, we've gone out a few times, but *no*, it's not like that. We're just friends."

Jace wanted to believe his buddy, but wasn't inclined to trust that the lady magnet could go out with a woman on a strictly friendship basis. Females of all ages found the elusive cowboy irresistible.

"It's true," Harper insisted, then punctuated with a burp. "I've seen them parasailing several times this summer. If Tanner was getting a piece of that, then he wouldn't have kept going out with her. You know how he has that three date rule, Captain."

His teeth were still clenched tight over the "getting a piece of that" remark, but began to loosen as the truth of the rest of the statement sunk in. His buddy was the biggest commitment-phobe of the bunch. If the relationship avoider had been seen with Holly the whole summer, then there definitely wasn't any sex involved. Time and again, he'd watched Tanner cross that threshold, but after the third date, the loner walked away.

At least his friend was upfront with the women he dated. Jace wouldn't have been friends with him for the past decade, otherwise. And since he had a similar rule, they got along fine. They also never dated the same woman. So, if Tanner was seeing, or had seen Holly in that sense, then Jace would steer clear, jolt or no jolt.

That's if he was inclined to pursue the woman with the hands-off attitude, which he wasn't.

Although, lately, he didn't need a rule. He didn't date. Sure, there had been plenty of opportunities, but between work at the co-op practice, helping his mother and sister on the ranch, and his weekends with the guard, he had no time for a social life.

"Why does it matter, anyway, Jace?" Tanner stared at him from across the table with that serious brown gaze that had new recruits, both in the guard and at the firehouse, shaking in their boots. "You're resigning your commission come spring, right? Or did you change your mind?"

Harper's head snapped up. "Really, Cap? You're leaving the guard?"

He nodded. “Yeah, it’s time.” Now that his contract with the National Guard was under the one year mark, he planned to leave Harland County next May.

Another reason to avoid getting involved with a woman now.

“You’re joining Doctors Without Borders,” Jesse stated in his trademark quiet tone.

Again, he nodded. “Yes. My mom and sister seemed to be settling into a good routine and should be able to handle the ranch while I’m gone.”

He’d always planned to join the humanitarian organization that provided medical care to nearly seventy countries worldwide, saving lives threatened by violence, catastrophe, or neglect, and treating people regardless of race, politics, or religion. Since he’d encountered the group in Iraq, that drive had grown even stronger.

But, he’d put off his plan to join DWB for a few years now. Ever since his HIV positive father had died from complication of pneumonia four years ago while Jace had been on deployment. His father contracting the virus through a blood transfusion after a car accident when Jace had been ten was the reason he became a doctor with the intent to help others around the world live with the disease.

But not until things were good at home. His sister’s riding accident this past June had jeopardized his plans.

“How is Lacey?” Harper asked. “That was a terrible spill she took.”

“Yeah, it was, but she was lucky,” he replied, setting down his empty cup. “So far, the fracture in her back is healing nicely. She’ll finish therapy at the end of next month.”

“It’s a miracle she’s walking,” Tanner stated.

It was a miracle she wasn't dead.

He shook off the dark thoughts and forced air into his lungs. She'd suffered a fractured back between the second and third vertebrae, miraculously hadn't broken her neck or had bone in the spinal canal requiring surgery.

At twenty-four, Lacey was headstrong, and the apparent fantasy of too many of his Guard buddies, reminding him of Jordan McCall. Come hell or high-water, she said she'd walk again, and by God, she accomplished that within the first five weeks. He was damn proud of his sister, but she needed to pace herself.

"I just wish she'd slow down and not take so many damn chances."

"Don't think she's made that way, Doc," Jesse observed with an undercurrent in his sarcastic tone.

Jace wondered if something was going on between his sister and the quiet guardsman who sometimes helped out at the ranch, along with Tanner and their friend Kade Dalton. If so, the man was going to have his hands full, because whoever captured his sister's heart needed to be made of some stern stuff.

"I heard that," Harper drawled, chucking his cup in the trash. "Now, who's up for another set?"

Everyone rose in response.

"Whose turn is it to pay?" Tanner asked, tossing out his cup.

Jesse frowned. "Didn't you?"

"Nope. I just put in the order. It's not my turn to pay."

The rest grumbled, *"Me either,"* and scattered away, leaving Jace alone with his grinning friend. He shook his head.

"Thanks, Jace." Tanner slapped him on the back and joined the already shirtless jerks on the beach.

He maneuvered around the outdoor tables and headed toward The Creamery. "Like I had a choice."

The guys often let him pick up the tab. They, like most people, assumed because he was a doctor he had a lot of money. Not true. He was still paying student loans. His father had wanted to take out a second mortgage on the ranch, but he refused. Another bill was the last thing his family had needed. After years of struggling to make ends meet, his father had finally been out from under a mound of medical bills. Jace saw no reason to replace them with another mortgage. Harland County had a lot of ranches, and he'd worked on every one of them to help put himself through schooling. That and the Texas National Guard. He'd joined ten years ago to help pay for his education. He was finally getting his footing. His mom and sister were set financially, and he was turning the corner on his finances.

The time had come to pursue his future and face new challenges.

But first, he had to pay for the smoothies, which worked for him because he wanted to apologize to the green-eyed bombshell, anyway.

A voice inside his head told him not to bother, that Holly had a strong backbone and could handle his teasing, but his moral compass wouldn't allow him to go about his day without making amends.

He just hoped she'd listen.

As he walked toward the window, he noted several customers and decided to go inside instead of waiting in line. Besides, he needed a little relief from the heat.

As he stepped inside the vacant shop, he was hit by the blessed cold of the air conditioner…and globs of flying ice cream, followed by Holly's panicked voice.

"*Donny!*"

Chapter Two

Unable to avoid a second hit, Jace took a smattering to the face and ear. The sticky, cold substance slid down his neck while he ducked to evade a third, taking cover behind a display case.

"It won't shut off," the young college student yelled, jamming button after button.

Ice cream covered the ceiling, walls, and floors in a pink, organic hue, dripping off The Creamery's three unlucky occupants.

Holly lunged for the outlet, managing to yank the cord from the wall while she slipped on a milkshake puddle by her feet. The whirl of a blender dissipated, along with the flying dessert, both giving way to a muttered oath as the valiant woman smashed into a work table on her way to the floor; the clang of bowls and spoons echoed in the suddenly quiet shop.

Jace sprang into action, locking the door to prevent customers from coming into the war zone, then slip-slided his way behind the counter to the grumbling proprietor and her clueless employee.

"Donny, go finish your order at the window," he directed. "And be careful where you walk."

"But…" The young man blinked down at his boss who sat on the floor cradling her left elbow.

"I'll take care of her. Now, go."

"Yes, sir." The young man poured what was left of the milkshake into a cup and tip-toed back to the grinning customer at the window.

"That was awesome, man."

Jace's mind registered the teenage customer's proclamation as he made his way to the injured woman. She blinked up at him, those gorgeous green eyes switching from dazed to amused before she burst out laughing. Deciding it was better than her bursting into tears, he smiled and knelt down in front of her.

"Do I look as bad as you?" she asked between laughs.

Ice cream plastered dark bangs to her forehead, dripping onto the beauty's face and off her chin to slide down a delectable chest and disappear between mouthwatering cleavage. She looked positively delicious, and he had to fight the urge to lean forward and lick her clean.

"Worse," he replied with a grin.

"Gee, thanks." She snickered and made to get up.

He cupped her shoulder and gently pushed her back down. "Easy, there, chuckles. That was some fall. Let me check you out."

"I'm fine." She swatted his hands away, tried to push off the floor, then winced.

He blew out a breath. *Damn, stubborn woman.* "Sure you are." Ignoring her grumble, he gently, but thoroughly, examined her arm.

"Ouch." She jerked back when he reached her elbow.

He knew from months of watching her with her uncle, and here at work, that she could handle tough situations without a crease in her brow or complaint on her tempting lips. So, for the competent woman to cry out from his light touch, she was in a lot of pain.

"You hit the table pretty hard. You should have it x-rayed."

She cocked her head and smiled tight. "The table's fine."

He leveled the exasperating woman with one of his stern looks. The kind he gave to the soldiers in his platoon. At least they had the good sense to look contrite. Not Holly. *Hell no.* She just continued to stare unblinkingly through those damn, gorgeous eyes of hers.

"That's not what I meant and you know it," he said, a little more than tired of her mistrust. A mistrust she only appeared to reserve just for him. She was outright friendly and even smiled with her eyes to his friends.

Her chin rose, her gaze less than tolerant. "I can't leave the shop."

"Then let me finish my exam."

After a brief moment of hesitation, she held out her arm, and he quickly got back to evaluating before she changed her mind. After finding no disconnect, or evidence of a fracture, he grabbed a nearby dish towel and fashioned a sling. "It doesn't appear to be broken, and since you won't get it x-rayed, try to keep your arm immobile for a few days."

She snorted. "Not gonna happen, Doc. I need to drive."

"Not if it hurts," he replied, leaning closer. "I'm serious." The last thing he needed was to worry about the headstrong woman behind the wheel of a car with an injured arm.

"I know, but so am I," she insisted. "My uncle has an appointment with the orthopedic specialist this Wednesday and my mother doesn't drive. No way are we missing that." She glanced down at her arm. "I'm sure it'll be fine in a day or two. I just whacked my funny bone, that's all."

He wasn't so sure. And there was nothing funny about her getting hurt.

She tried to get up again, so he hooked a hand under her other arm and brought them both to their feet, careful of the slop on the floor.

"Come by my office on Tuesday, and I'll reexamine you."

She pulled free and grumbled. "Thanks…and no thanks. I'll be fine."

Donny chose that moment to tip-toe back over. "I'm so sorry, boss. I have no idea what happened. The darn lid wouldn't stay on, and next I knew, Raspberry Supreme was flying all over the place. Then I tried, but I couldn't get any of the buttons to work—"

"It's okay," she reassured, expression softening as she addressed the contrite kid. "I should've warned you about it. You just take care of the customers at the window while I clean up."

"Will do, boss." Donny smiled and headed back to his station, relief sagging his slight shoulders.

It was at that moment, Jace realized the woman sometimes looked at him with heat in her gaze, but never warmth. And, son-of-a-bitch, he wondered just what he had to do to change that outcome.

Less than amused with her less than friendly attitude, he stepped closer, and when she backed up, he followed, until a counter blocked her escape. "Tell me…*Holly*." He deliberately used her first name, and heaven help him, he liked how it rolled off his tongue, and the way desire darkened her gaze in response. "Do you dislike all doctors, or is it just me?"

Her lips parted and chest rose in an enticement almost too much to bear. Then her throaty, sexy voice met his ear.

"All doctors."

Heat skittered down his spine, and he had to fight the urge to lean in and kiss her trembling mouth.

Instead, he ran a finger through the ice cream on her cheek, then licked it off, wishing he could put his mouth on her. "As long as it's not me."

She shrugged, her gaze full of mistrust. And heat.

He chuckled. She was a tough nut to crack, one he should avoid, but knew he wouldn't. After fishing the wallet out of the back pocket of his shorts, he set money on the counter behind the suddenly still woman, then held her gaze, eager to see what she did next.

"This is for the smoothies. Thanks for the delicious...*desserts*."

Need flared in her green gaze and dilated the pupils in her fathomless eyes. A powerful jolt of arousal shot down his spine and zinged his favorite body parts to life. Parts he ignored, except in the shower after waking up hard from a dream she'd haunted.

"You're welcome," she replied with a hint of reproach in her tone that signified he wasn't about to get any other type of dessert from her. "And thanks for tending to my arm, Doc."

He nodded and stepped back, wiping his face on a towel she handed him. If she didn't want to act on whatever was zipping between them, then so be it. He never forced himself on a woman in his life. They tended to seek him out.

"Just make sure you stop by in a few days so I can take another look," he said, dropping the towel on the counter while he held her gaze. "But if it starts to swell, or the pain increases, you get your stubborn...*elbow* to the emergency room." He caught himself just in time, and kept his orders impersonal. Despite the little bit of teasing, he wanted her to take the situation serious and not ignore his advice.

She nodded as she carefully made her way to the register in a blatant attempt to get rid of him. “Will do, Doc.”

If he hadn’t been watching her, he would’ve sworn she’d saluted him.

“How about I help you clean up. Gonna be kind of hard with one hand.”

“Naw. I can manage.” She shrugged and cracked a smile that almost reached her eyes. “Here’s your change. Sorry about the extra milkshake.”

One of the most effective doctoring skills in his arsenal was his ability to read people, and Holly was coming across loud and clear. She was tired, in pain, and on edge, that last part because of him. He seemed to push her to that boundary just as she pushed him. He didn’t know what the hell to do about that, or even if he should.

“No problem.” He held his hand out for his money and watched the woman pull her bottom lip between her teeth the moment her finger brushed his palm. Another damn zing traveled straight to his groin.

A tight jaw contradicted the heat in her gaze, and stirred more than his curiosity. Just what had happened to her to forge a dislike of doctors? And did she taste as exquisite as she looked?

Then, not for the first time, he wondered why the hell it mattered since he was not looking for a romantic relationship.

Just as he was about to turn and leave, a glob of ice cream dropped from the ceiling and splattered onto her head. She jumped back and shrieked, and the movement caused the mixture to slide down her face and drip onto her already deliciously coated chest.

He knew better than to laugh, no matter how adorable she appeared, pink goop dripping off her exasperated face. Muttering under her breath, she reached below the counter, pulled out another dish towel and wiped her face.

Her choppy ministrations managed to smear more than eradicate.

He stepped closer, and using the corner of the towel still in her hand, he gently dabbed at her lower lip. She stilled, and appeared to stop breathing.

Oxygen seemed to have a hard time making it into his lungs, too. "You missed a spot." He wiped her chin, and another speck by her ear.

"Thanks," she whispered, then swallowed, her gaze dropping to his mouth.

This time, he stilled.

All the cold air from the air conditioner seemed to disappear, leaving heat. Lots of heat. Jace was torn about what to do. It was the middle of the day, in the middle of her shop. Definitely not appropriate for crushing her close and tasting that trembling lower lip of hers for himself. But he couldn't get his body to move away. In fact, they seemed to be closer, which had to come from her, because he'd remained still, not wanting to jeopardize what little progress he'd made with his attempt to prove some doctors could be trusted.

Her gaze traveled up to meet his, and she blinked, staring at him like she'd only really just seen him. Then suddenly, their breath mingled, and he had no idea how they'd gotten so close he could count the green hues in her eyes. Three. There were three shades, each melting into the other, and he empathized, ready to chuck common sense and take what the beautiful woman was offering.

"Yo! Jace? I can see you. What's up? You playing doctor in there or what? Why the hell is the door locked?" Tanner asked, banging on said locked door.

Holly jumped back with a startled gasped.

"I'll unlock it," he said, turning around and heading to let his vociferous pal inside.

Along with the rest of the grinning volleyball crew.

"What in the world were you doing in here? Having an ice cream fight?" Tanner frowned, tipping his head to peer up at the ceiling. "And you didn't invite us?"

Harper snickered. "This some new kind of foreplay?"

Color rose up Holly's neck and flooded her cheeks, rivaling the pink splattered around the stark white and sky blue room.

"Yeah, you two looked awfully cozy when we got to the door." One of the other guys smiled. "Sorry to interrupt."

"The only thing you interrupted was me giving Doctor Turner his change," Holly said, lifting her chin so high you'd swear she had a nosebleed.

Unsure if she'd welcome his help, he decided he didn't care, he was giving it just the same. Straightening his spine, he stared the guys down. "Not that it's any of your business, but Donny had a slight mishap with the blender, and I was helping Ms. Phillips clean up. How about you can the teasing and pitch in?"

"It's my fault." The beet red employee stepped away from the window to face the men. "Darn lid blew off the blender and now the raspberry milkshake is all over the store, and Holly slipped and hurt her arm."

The smile disappeared from everyone's faces as they eyed the make-shift sling around the blushing woman's neck. Jokes put aside, the men snapped to attention before springing into action. Harper re-locked the door. Jesse and the two others headed behind the counter toward the storage closet, and Tanner, hell,

Tanner made a beeline straight for his parasailing buddy.

Before Jace could.

"We'll get this cleaned up, Hol." Like a seasoned rescuer, the guy led her by her good arm to a clean chair in the corner. "Just sit there and leave this to us."

"Okay. Thanks." Damn woman smiled up at Tanner. And it reached her eyes, too.

Jace rubbed at his tight chest. Not two minutes ago, she'd refused his offer to help. Of course, none of the other guys were doctors. But dwelling on it solved nothing. She needed help, and he was going to take advantage of her permission.

Fifteen minutes later, working as a unit, he and the guys had the place spotless and reopened for business, only having to tell her twice to sit down. He studied her as she rose to her feet and headed back behind the counter. She didn't appear to be ticked-off at having been made to sit back while they'd cleaned. In fact, she smiled a genuine smile and even directed it at him.

All the air seemed to be sucked from the room. He stared, mesmerized at the light sparkling in her gaze.

So damn gorgeous.

"Free dessert for everyone," she announced.

Woots went up around the room.

"As long as it's not a milkshake." Tanner winked, and poor Donny blushed at his stance by the window.

She smiled at her employee. "I'm sure Donny can handle it this time. And once our industrial machine is repaired, we can put the darn blender back in storage."

As the guys placed their orders, Jace continued to stare at the beauty. A strange feeling rippled through his chest. The woman's fierce conviction and support for a friend sparked his admiration. At times, she was a puzzle, and others, an open book.

It was common knowledge he was addicted to both.

Thanks to the past half-hour, he knew, without a doubt, tonight he'd dream about the enticing woman, and about licking ice cream off her curves with thorough precision.

Holly had had high hopes this would be her last week in Harland County—until the orthopedic surgeon announced Uncle Arthur had had a setback thanks to a fall he suffered during the night.

While her mom accompanied her uncle for an x-ray, Holly walked blindly down the hall, fighting a strong sense of panic. The building was full of doctors' offices and labs, but what she really needed was some air. Her chest was tight, throat closing. She could feel her prized job slipping through her damn fingers.

This can't be happening.

Sagging against the window at the end of the corridor, she gazed out at the sea of blue bonnets scattered around the grounds. Their beauty brought little solace today. "I can't believe I'm going to be stuck here."

"What's wrong with here?"

Holly jumped and swung around at the sound of Jace's voice. "You shouldn't sneak up on people." Hand over her thudding heart, she stared at the approaching man. "It's impolite."

"Sorry. Didn't mean to offend you," he said, coming to a stop in front of her, a walking advertisement for fluttering heartbeats in navy pants and charcoal sweater over a light blue, button-down shirt.

Her heart dutifully fluttered.

"My office is in there, remember?" He pointed to the door on her immediate left. "I was just coming back from lunch. Are you okay? You sounded a little distraught."

She snorted, then sobered. "I guess I am a little." She hadn't even realized her footsteps had taken her toward his practice.

"What's wrong? Is it your uncle?" He reached out to lightly touch her shoulder, and the warmth of his palm spread a tingly heat throughout her body.

It felt…nice.

"Yes, well, not completely." Kind of like her. She wasn't completely okay either. With her uncle issues. Her employment issues. Her Jace issues. "He apparently thought he was well enough to make a three a.m. bathroom run without waking my mother."

"Ah hell."

He released her and blew out a breath, then stared at her with those compassionate blue eyes of his. The one's that saw right through the barriers and seared into her soul.

"You look like you could use a coffee. Come inside my office."

She nodded and allowed him to usher her past his reception to his office in back. It had been too tiring a morning to keep him at bay and refuse his offer. Coffee was definitely in order. And since his waiting room had been empty, she didn't feel too guilty taking up a little of his time. "Thanks. I hope I'm not keeping you from work, though."

"No." He shook his head and smiled. "My next appointment isn't for another half-hour, so I'm all yours until then."

Her pulse stuttered, and it took her a second to form a thought to reply. "Oh."

Maybe she should've taken two seconds.

"How do you want your coffee?"

"Black."

He opened his office door and waited for her to step inside before he nodded. "I'll be right back."

Holly let out a breath and glanced around the familiar room, taking a closer look. The bookcase behind his big desk was loaded with medical journals and matched the dark wood of his furniture. Two plush, brown leather arm chairs sat in front of his desk, and matched the couch along the back wall, big enough to sleep two. Floor to ceiling window's lined the south wall, letting in a wonderful, natural light, while a dusty blue paint covered the other walls that housed a myriad of framed degrees, awards, and photos.

Like a moth to a flame, she drew closer, a combination of her obsession over photographs…and him. Several pictures showed the sexy man dressed in a suit, receiving awards, standing with his arm around two women she assumed were his mother and sister, going by the startling resemblance of dark hair and blue eyes. A few were of him in fatigues and in full battle gear with a bunch of soldiers.

Holly recognized Tanner and the volleyball guys, and Kade Dalton, whom she knew was Jace's good friend. The comradery and kinship mirrored on their faces, and in one photo of just him and Kade, she saw more than she wanted.

Pain.

A shared pain. Their eyes were full of it, even though their mouths were turned up in a smile. Her heart clutched. Which wasn't good. She didn't want to feel anything for this man. It was bad enough a strong attraction simmered between them. At least she could try to fight that; hell, she had been ever since stepping foot in this very office with her uncle and mother all those months ago.

"Black coffee as ordered."

She jumped and twisted to find Jace walking into the room, two cups in his hands. "Th-thanks." Heat rushed into her face as if he'd caught her watching him strip naked.

Heat of a different kind rushed south with rapid force.

He glanced from her to the photos, then back before handing her a coffee. "My secretary insists I put them up there. Says it makes me more accessible to the patients."

"I think she's right." She liked the middle-aged woman who ran the office. Linda was efficient and personable, with a good head for business. The fact she'd forced him to put his achievements on display, proved it. "I think this photo is my favorite."

Sipping her drink, she enjoyed the warmth as it slid down her throat then pointed to a picture of the doctor wearing fatigues. He stood in a village with a little girl in his arms, a small boy hugging his legs, and a young couple holding another little boy. The smiles on their faces were so genuine, she felt their gratitude straight through the lens.

"That was during our last deployment."

His gaze settled on the photo, and she watched satisfaction and pure joy spread across his face. Breath caught in her throat. His whole demeanor, even his posture transformed. He stood taller; smile broadening, he lit up from within. She couldn't take her eyes off him as he continued to stare at the picture.

"We were passing through a village and ran across a group from Doctors Without Borders that needed some help. This family's little girl is HIV positive. I had the privilege of educating them on little things they could do to help her live with the disease."

His passion for the subject ruled his features and was so strong, she could feel it vibrating within him. Holly remained silent, sipped her coffee and listened as he told her about the village. She tried to comprehend the difference between him and her father. And ex-boyfriend. Jace seemed to truly care about people, whereas all her father cared about was money. And her ex about himself.

He turned and caught her staring at him. "What?" A grin tugged his lips. "You're looking at me as if I've grown two heads."

Two hearts, maybe. Or one big one the size of two. Was he for real? A gorgeous, compassionate doctor? He couldn't be real.

Right?

She blinked and blindly pointed to another photo in an attempt to change the subject. "What about this one?"

His knowing gaze narrowed, but he cut her some slack and turned his attention to the picture. Then stilled.

It was only a minuscule movement, but she noticed, along with the tightening in his jaw and the way the light dimmed from his eyes.

"That was from this last deployment, too."

She waited for him to elaborate about the photo with Kade, but after a few silent beats passed, she decided to nudge further, refusing to dissect why it mattered. "You lost someone."

Another minuscule movement. A slight nod. "Sergeant Nylan. Shayla's fiancé."

Her chin shot up. "Oh. Amelia's father." She'd wondered about him, but had never asked. It wasn't any of her business, and if her friend had wanted to talk, she'd listen. If not, that was fine, too.

What wasn't fine, was the dark expression on the handsome doctor's face as he continued to stare at the photo, when just a few minutes ago, he could've lit the night. Even though she didn't want to pester, she just couldn't let him dwell in that dark place. "If it brings back a bad memory, why leave it up?"

For some reason, the thought of him being transported back to that moment over and over, bothered her more than it should. Which made no sense. Heck, they weren't even technically friends. And yet, it did bother her, laying like a piece of lead in her stomach.

"I leave it up there to remind me I'm not infallible. That I can't save everyone. That I'm…"

"Human," she whispered, throat suddenly too tight to breath.

"Yeah."

Once again, her mind tried to comprehend the man. A doctor. Who cared about people. She knew that was technically what doctors were supposed to do, but in her experience, it tipped the other way. Big time. In her experience, the title often meant more than the oath taken.

Doctor Jace Turner was human. And that made him so very dangerous. She liked humans. She liked him. Which was such a bad idea, because she wasn't staying in Harland County.

So, why the hell was she leaning closer to the man who was leaning closer to her?

Because she was an idiot.

Holly drew back, then swiveled around and marched to the window, bringing her cup to her lips. Coffee was cold. She was hot. A hysterical giggle bubbled up her throat. No. She was in control. Time to switch the subject back to the reason she had accepted his offer in the first place.

Her uncle.

"The orthopedic surgeon said my uncle's fall caused a setback. He's being x-rayed now." Her mom blamed herself for not helping. Her uncle blamed himself for not asking his sister for help, and Holly blamed the stars for not aligning in her plight to leave Texas.

She heard a small thunk and deduced it to be his empty cup hitting the bottom of his garbage can.

"What about you?" he asked, catching her off guard.

"Wh-what about me?"

"How's your elbow? You never did stop by to see me."

"It's good. See?" She moved her arm all around to show him she was fine and pain free.

Guess it wasn't good enough for him because he stepped close and began to examine her arm with two big, warm hands.

The heat of arousal flickered to life, and she fought back a tremor. "I kept it immobile like you said for two days. Not with the dish towel." She laughed. "Tanner brought me a sling."

"Of course he did."

His voice was dry, and she longed to see his expression, but his head was down as he concentrated on her arm. "Looks like you got lucky. Just don't try to push it."

Not her style. *Okay, yes, yes it was*. But not when it came to health issues.

She downed the last of her cold coffee. "Don't worry. I won't. Unlike my uncle."

He released her and met her gaze with a frown. "Is he in a lot of pain?"

"A little," she replied. "His knee hurts, not his hip."

"I'm sorry. I know you were hoping to leave this week."

She nodded, but didn't glance at him, uncaring if it was rude. It was safe, and that was more important.

"What will happen with your job?"

His voice was full of the compassion she knew she'd see shining in his eyes…if she chucked safe in the trash along with her empty coffee and turned to face him.

She didn't. Just walked to the can, tossed the cup, and stared at the crumpled heap.

"It's for a ski resort, right?"

Realizing he was waiting for a reply, she drew in a breath and shot from the hip. "Yeah, it is, and I don't know what's going to happen." Her heart lurched at the thought. "They'll probably give the position to whoever has been filling in for me."

Saying it out loud increased the pain in her chest. And now her eyes were leaking. "Dammit." She twisted her back to him and swiped at her wet cheeks. "Family comes first. It was just a stupid job."

"Hey, no, it's not stupid," he said, suddenly standing in front of her, warm hand on her shoulder while the other tipped her chin to force her to meet his understanding gaze. "Even I know how much the job means to you."

"You do? How?"

"During your uncle's last appointment, your mother told me how hard you worked for that promotion," he replied.

The compassion softening his voice and gaze did funny things to her pulse.

"It's not over until they say it is, and even then, you fight for it. You should never give up on your dreams, Holly. Never."

She hiccupped. Her dreams? Hell, it had been so long since she indulged in something so...*frivolous*, as her father used to call it, she wasn't sure how anymore.

He stilled, and bent at the knee to look her straight in the eyes. "This wasn't your dream job?"

Her brain was having trouble connecting thoughts, thanks to the cells he was zapping with his electrifying touch. Little tingles raced down her arm and spine. Her mind was stuck on the fact her skin felt fused where they touched. And she liked it.

Dammit.

"Holly?"

"Yeah?" She blinked, but it didn't help. He was so close she could smell his woodsy aftershave, mixed with man, and she had all she could do not to lean forward and inhale.

And maybe lick.

"What is your dream job?"

She shrugged. "I-I don't know." Her brain was still focused on the licking thing. She forced herself to speak. "When I was in high school, I had wanted to go to college to pursue photography." She waited for his laugh, or snide remark about her impromptu photo shoot of him and the other shirtless guys playing volleyball, but he didn't say a word, or crack a smile. He just stared at her with those incredible eyes that saw everything. "But, my father said it was impractical, and he wouldn't help financially."

"I'm sorry."

His frown created three creases across his forehead, and she concentrated on them while she shrugged again. "My mom didn't have any kind of money." *Not after putting my jerk father through school.*

The kind woman had struggled to make ends meet most of their lives. Sure, her dad paid alimony and child support, but he'd gotten a great lawyer, so the payments were bare minimal. Her mother had eventually remarried a nice man. A blue-collar worker. The last thing Holly had wanted was to put the financial burden of college loans on them. They never had much money, but they were happy until the day he died.

"I knew I needed a good job to help pay for my brother's college someday, so I decided to major in business and marketing. I figured that was a broad enough field to keep me employed for the rest of my life."

"You shouldn't have to settle. Ever."

His thumb was tracing her lower lip now, and she was so totally on board with how wonderful it made her feel, all hot and toasty and so very alive. She found if she nodded, his thumb covered more of her lip.

He sucked in a breath before he cupped her face with both hands and stepped closer. The movements brought so much of his delicious body in contact with hers, she was on sensory overload. He was hot and hard, and she felt herself melting.

"Holly." His voice was low and deliciously sexy.

Her mind had just enough juice left to send out a weak warning she needed to step back and refrain from lip-locking with the doc. But, her wires got crossed, and she ended up stepping forward instead.

Chapter Three

Twice in less than a week.

When Jace had offered Holly a cup of coffee, he hadn't planned to get so close to the woman they'd share a breath. First at her job, and now at his. The woman killed his restraint. Every. Damn. Time.

He couldn't let go. Couldn't step back, even though his mind insisted he gave the distance thing another shot. For the first time since he'd known her, she was open with him, allowing a glimpse of the real Holly Phillips. He liked what he saw. Not just the body melting into his, all soft and warm, but the heart visible in her open gaze.

She was a good woman who sacrificed for family, and felt the same crazy pull of attraction turning him inside out. Her heart raced and pulse beat erratic at the base of her throat, and when he backed her up against the desk, her hands reached out to palm his chest while her teeth sank into the plump of her lower lip. Need spiked a path straight to his groin. He wanted to bite and sooth and lick.

Every inch of her.

Her hair was silky soft under his hands, and she smelled as sweet as the desserts she concocted in her uncle's shop. Erotic images from his dreams flashed through his mind, and heat spread out in tight formation to every zone in his body. This time, there would be no retreat.

He lowered his mouth, sharing another breath, giving her a chance to back away.

Hands, warm and a little desperate, tightened their hold on his chest as she lifted up on tiptoe in an open invitation.

Loud and clear. He got the message, and acting accordingly, he kissed her. The soft moan rumbling up her throat blazed through him like wildfire.

He *knew* it. For months, he'd wondered if she'd taste as incredible as his dreams.

Even better.

Her hands were in his hair now, holding him as if she was afraid he'd leave. Hell no. Not now that he'd finally gotten her where he'd wanted all these months. In his arms.

Jace deepened the kiss, opening his mouth on her wider, acquainting himself with her sweet taste, enjoying the soft little sounds coming from her throat, full of need and surprise.

He could feel her heart pounding hard in her chest. Or was that his? Didn't matter. The mistrust and wariness were gone. She let him in. Pressed closer, held tighter, murmured his name against his lips, wanting more. Well hell, he had a lot more to give.

Warning bells clanged in his head. He was treading dangerous waters, in deep, deeper than he'd been in years. It didn't matter. She felt incredible. Tasted amazing, and he ignored his brain.

Tipping her head, he changed the angle of the kiss and took everything she gave. The veracity of her hunger blew brain cell after brain cell. He needed more. A hell of a lot more. Trailing his hands down her throat to her shoulders—

"Doctor Turner." His secretary's voice filled the room. "We have an emergency patient who requires stitches."

He went still, then drew back with a curse, partly for his lost opportunity, and partly because he was taking liberties in his office he should not be taking. Either way, he walked over to hit the button to reply. "Put the patient in examining room two. I'll be right there."

"Okay."

He turned to find Holly had moved. She stood near the door.

"Thanks for the coffee," she said, gaze no longer warm and open as he approached. "I should get going."

Back in safe mode.

Probably for the better.

Neither of them were staying in Texas. Hell, she could be gone by next weekend. And he was definitely leaving in the spring. Kissing her had been foolish. Acting on their attraction had been foolhardy.

And yet, he couldn't keep from reaching out to cup her face. Damn, she was soft, and those eyes, so green and…wary.

She stepped back, her hand fumbling for the door knob. "I-I have to go, and you have a patient to see."

Her reminder brought a curse to his lips. How the hell had he forgotten that already? The woman was too damn dangerous to his thought process.

"Hope your uncle's x-rays turn out okay," he said, gently brushing her fingers aside and opening the door.

A blush rushed up into her cheeks, enhancing her mesmerizing gaze, and upping his pulse.

"Me, too," she muttered, before she rushed down the corridor and yanked open the waiting room door.

Turning in the opposite direction toward the patient bleeding in exam room two, he lectured his body to simmer down and not think about the woman's sexy sashay or sweet, heated taste.

It didn't listen.

He adjusted himself, not wanting to give the patient a good view of the boner holding out hope Holly would play doctor, before he opened the door.

Although Harland County was big, Jace knew just about everyone, having gone to school or served in the Texas Guard with someone from each local family, including the McCalls. He'd been a few years ahead of Kerri in school, and a few years behind her husband. Connor was a big, tall, broad cattle rancher, and best friends with his buddy Kade. The cowboy was also dusty, sweaty, and bleeding.

"What's up, Doc?"

He smiled, and relaxed as he rushed forward to hug Kerri and shake Connor's hand. "Hi, you two. What's going on?"

A quick assessment of the situation, and the dust and blood on the back of Connor's torn T-shirt, told him the tall cowboy was his stitching recipient. Which was good, considering Kerri was in the first trimester of pregnancy. The smiling woman was a little pale, but otherwise, appeared in good health.

He turned to her husband. "You have a fight with a fence, Connor?"

"Yeah, you break the cow's rules, the cow will make you pay. Kind of like my wife." The rancher chuckled, then winced when said wife punched his arm, then jammed her hands on her hips.

"Are you calling me a cow?"

"What?" The big guy's voice squeaked. "No! Hell no. You're the most beautiful woman in the world, darlin'." He rushed to grab her hands, wincing, no doubt from stretching his cuts.

Her chin lifted slightly, and Jace would've believed Kerri's indignation was real if not for the smile tugging her lips. "Go on."

"In the whole universe, and I'm damn lucky to have you."

The cowboy was smart, and knew how to kiss ass.

And still bleeding.

"And I'd like to check out your wound," he said, motioning for the giant to have a seat on the examining table. "How exactly did the cow make you pay?"

"She didn't like to be told what to do. Kind of like…" Connor paused and glanced at his wife, who narrowed her eyes from her perch on a chair. "Like the other cows in the heard. She just got a little overzealous when we tagged her, and she nudged me backward into the fence. I tried to tell my wife I just needed a Band-Aid, but she insisted on bringing me here."

"It was either here or the ER, bucko," Kerri stated, chin lifting again, this time, minus the grin.

Jace helped Connor take off what was left of his shirt, then eyed the jagged slices of skin near the cowboy's left shoulder blade. "Your wife is also smart. You're going to need more than a Band-Aid, I'm afraid."

"Then use the whole damn box, Doc. I don't care."

"Sure," he said, heading to the cupboard to fetch a stitch kit. "Right after I put the stitches in."

"Stitches? Ah, hell. Is that really necessary?" The brown-haired cowboy's face turned a little pale.

He moved to the sink and began to clean up. "Yep. A dozen or two."

"Can't you glue it? I have some super gorilla stuff back at the ranch. That glue is tough. I'll go get it."

Shaking his head, Jace dried his hands. "Sorry. The area of the wound is too broad."

Connor's posture became stiffer with each passing second. "This isn't going to work, Doc. Needles and I…we don't get along," he exclaimed, eyeing the door.

"Don't even think it, cowboy," Kerri said, rising to her feet as Jace grabbed antiseptic, sterile water, and gauze. "Just let Doctor Turner do his job so we can get out of here."

Her husband's brows rose in anticipation. "Maybe stop by The Creamery?"

"Yeah." The brilliant woman nodded. "I'd like that."

Jace would like that, too. He was envious just knowing they might see Holly if she was done with her uncle. How pathetic was that?

Very.

He irrigated the wound free of dirt and impurities, damn impressed the cowboy hadn't winced or hissed once during the process that had to hurt like a bitch. He nodded to Kerri who kept her husband talking while Jace grabbed the needle encasement and opened it on the table. Before the giant could turn around and spy what he was doing, he drew Lidocaine into the syringe, flicked a finger at the needle to shake out the excess air, then began to inject the numbing agent into the wound.

The cowboy stilled, and tried to turn his head to see what he was doing. "You still cleaning back there, Doc?"

"Still working on it," he replied with a slight fib, pulling the needle out and sticking it in another area. "How many ears did you tag today?"

Connor went on to recount his day, and by the time he finished, Jace tied the last stitch, set the curved needle on the tray, then carried it to the counter. His patient twisted around, glanced at the tray and turned sheet white.

"*Jesus*, Doc. Did you stick that needle in me? Is that what you were doing back there?"

"Yep. You have seventeen stitches. Lucky seventeen," he said, bandaging the wound.

Smiling, Kerri rose to her feet. "And you didn't even flinch, sweetheart. I'm proud of you."

"Yeah?" The stiffness eased from the tense cowboy.

"Yeah."

A look of warmth and deep love passed between them, hitting Jace between the solar plexus. He'd never connected with a woman that way. He'd been too busy working, learning, deployed, taking care of his father, mother, and sister. It was during moments like this, when he saw two people headlong in love, that he wondered if he was missing out.

Which was dumb. He'd have enough time, after his stint abroad, to worry about finding someone special and settling down.

The image of a dark-haired beauty with clear, green eyes flashed through his mind, bringing her sweet taste with it.

"What do you say we get going?" Connor asked, rising to his feet.

"Hang on," he said, preparing another shot. "There was barbed wire in the fence."

"Yeah…so…" The giant backed up, eying the needle, face going a little green as he swallowed. "Now, don't go doing anything rash, Jace."

"Wouldn't dream of it," he replied.

"You managed the stitches just fine, sweetheart," Kerri reminded.

"That's because I didn't see them."

"Then close your eyes."

As the two debated, Jace made his move, swiping Connor's arm before sticking him.

"Son-of-a-bitch."

He helped the pale guy back to the table to sit down. "You're all done. As soon as you're up to it, you can go."

"Great." Connor drew in a few deep breaths. "You sure you don't wanna stick, scrape or probe anymore?"

"No, but…" Kerri stared from her husband to Jace, then back. "Tell him, Connor."

He stilled, switching his gaze between the married couple. "Tell me what?"

Shaking his head, the cowboy jumped to his feet, suddenly good to go. "I'm fine. It's just that flu going around or something."

The man hadn't said anything about not feeling well, and his skin hadn't been clammy or hot.

"Connor." Kerri stepped in front of her husband and blocked his exit, again. "It only happens whenever I'm nauseous."

Catching the meaning of her words, Jace had all he could do to hold back a grin. He'd read about legitimate cases, but never actually treated one. "You're saying you get sick whenever your wife does?"

After a moment's hesitation, Connor nodded.

"Any other issues?"

The cowboy ran a hand through his hair and blew out a breath. "Lately, I-I've been getting these strange cravings, Doc. It's ridiculous. Pickles and vanilla ice cream. Peanut butter and glazed donuts. What the hell is going on?"

Again, Jace had to fight to keep a straight face. The thought of this big, broad, barn of a man suffering pregnancy symptoms was a bit of a hoot. But, laughing would be unprofessional, so he bit the inside of his cheek and dropped the dirty equipment into the sink while he drew in a deep, deep breath before turning around.

"You're fine, Connor," he reassured with a straight face. "Once the baby arrives, all your strange cravings and impediments will go away."

"Ah…hell, Jace. Are you saying this is related to Kerri's pregnancy?"

"That's exactly what I'm saying."

Her snicker echoed around the room despite the hand she clamped over her mouth. Connor's gaze narrowed, first on his wife, then him.

"No. No, you're wrong. This is just a bug. A virus."

"Yeah, a nine-month one." Kerri giggled.

"Damn. If Cole ever finds out, or Kade…or, ah, hell, if Kevin…" He dropped onto the chair and stared at his dusty boots. "I'll never live this down. I'm doomed."

"They aren't going to find out, because we aren't going to say anything," Kerri stated as she pulled her husband to his feet.

"What about Jace?"

He stepped forward and shook his head. "Your secret's safe with me. You're my patient. I can't discuss patients with other people."

The cowboy released a breath and visibly relaxed, looking a lot less green. "Okay. Thanks." Then he frowned as if he thought of something. "You *are* my doctor, so as such, don't you have something I could take to get rid of these symptoms? I don't want them." Two big hands clamped down on his shoulders. "Make them go away, Doc. Give me a pill. I'll even take a shot. Just get rid of them."

The desperation in the man's voice and gaze made him consider lying. He didn't like to see his friend in distress, but believed in being truthful. "I can't. There's nothing to give. But, you should feel special, Connor. Very few men are so tuned into their wife's needs that they get to experience this journey together."

His patient turned to stare adoringly at his wife, and gently traced her flushed cheek. "I'll always know what you need, Kerri."

The warmth radiating from her smile was so sweet, yet in a way, painful to Jace, because it reminded him how empty his life was, again.

"Come on." She grabbed her husband's hand and kissed his knuckles. "Let's go to The Creamery. I'll share my pickle with you."

"Thanks, darlin'." He winked, dimples glaring. "It's only fair. I shared *mine* with you."

She punched the grinning cowboy's arm, again. "You goof. Behave, or I'll have the doctor give you another shot."

Jace laughed. "True. I could administer your antibiotics that way."

"Nope." Connor shook his head, dimples completely gone. "Just give me a prescription and I'll get out of your hair."

The ink was barely dry on the paper when it was yanked from his hands by the anxious man who promised to make an appointment to get the stitches taken out as he whisked his wife from the room.

With a smile tugging his lips, Jace cleaned up in a hurry. It was only a matter of time before his office was inundated with an influx of bruised females who had fainted at the sight of the shirtless, six-foot-four, cowboy that just left the building. His buddy always did leave a trail of swooning women.

If only he had that affect on a certain green-eyed beauty.

Chapter Four

Holly was surprised to find herself actually smiling and enjoying herself as she photographed the impromptu bridal shower for Shayla thrown by Caitlin, Brandi, and Kevin's sister Jen, catching the bride off guard by holding it at the McCalls' ranch on a Saturday.

Wild Creek had been hustling with activity for the outdoor party, giving it more of a cookout feel, thanks to unseasonably warm weather. Back home, they'd be discussing snow packs and powder in early October. It was strange to find herself wearing a dress and sandals, and equally strange to find she liked it.

A definite sign she'd been in south Texas too long. She hardly missed the start of the new snow season, celebrated the whole week, ending with a big outdoor bash, including bonfires and concerts.

She glanced down at her sandals and wiggled her toes, smirking at the mint green polish on the tips. Yeah, not something one would expose on a slope.

"I can't believe you all pulled this one over on me," Shayla said to her sister, Kerri, and Holly, as the four of them sat drinking iced tea at an empty table after the last guest had gone home. "I'm usually not so gullible."

"Why do you think we held it here at my place?" Kerri asked with a grin.

Caitlin nodded. "Yeah, sis, there was no way we could've surprised you with a bridal shower at Shadow Rock."

True. It had made more sense not to plan the surprise on the Dalton ranch where Shayla and her baby girl had moved the week after Kevin had proposed. She told her that Amelia was way too attached to her soon-to-be new daddy to wait until October.

Holly suspected it wasn't just the little girl who couldn't wait.

"I'm not so sure you couldn't have surprise me at home." Shayla snickered, rubbing her belly. "This baby seems to have sucked all the common sense from my brain lately."

"A sexy cowboy will do that, too," Kerri said, then promptly blushed.

Or a sexy doctor.

What the hell had she been thinking, kissing Jace in his office?

That was the problem. She *hadn't* been thinking. Not with her head, anyway. No, as soon as he drew near, touched her face, shared a breath, she had no coherent thought left in her muddled brain.

Her body sure hadn't complained. No. It had been all warm, and toasty, and tingly. Then he kissed her…well, maybe she sort of lifted up a little to meet him halfway. Okay, *all* the way, but he started it by getting so damn close.

Bugger had tasted even better than she'd imagined, and felt deliciously warm and solid and…

Holly realized the conversation had stopped, and the three women were staring at her, knowing grins on their faces.

"What?"

Shayla tipped her head and raised a brow. "When did it happen?"

"When did what happen?"

"The kiss you shared with Doctor Hottie."

Kerri nodded. "Yeah, we want details."

"All of them. I'm not getting any, so I need to live vicariously through the only other single female here," Caitlin insisted. "So, come on. Spill. Who kissed who first and where?"

"It wasn't that…not much happened," she finally said, stammering the whole time. Her mind was still trying to process the off-the-charts kiss.

Shayla's damn brow rose again. "I'm hearing the words, but your eyes tell another story."

She snorted. "Then you need glasses, because there is nothing to tell. We kissed. It was nice. I left." *On shaky legs, with a heart beating way out of control.* But they didn't need to know that part. Hell, she barely remembered leaving his office, or heading down the hall to her uncle's specialist. Just thinking about it now brought on the warm, tingly sensations the good doctor induced.

"Yeah, sure. You may have left, but that kiss certainly wasn't nothing. Your blush gives you away, honey," Shayla said, touching her arm. "It's okay. In fact, it's great. It's about damn time you two did something about the attraction simmering between you."

"I agree. Go for it." Caitlin nodded. "Don't let the fact you plan to leave Texas stop you from having some fun. I didn't let that stop me up in Pennsylvania, and I don't regret it."

"Really?"

She'd forgotten about her friend's dalliance. She eyed the grinning woman. Caitlin wasn't the type to have flings, and yet, she seemed to fair okay. Maybe she *was* making too much out of all the formality.

Nah. She couldn't just fall into bed with someone. It wasn't her, no matter how damn sexy the doctor was, or how sweet.

Holly blew out a breath and faced her cheering section. "Thanks. I know you mean well, but I think it's best if I keep my lips to myself for the rest of my stay in Harland County."

"Okay." Shayla held up her hands. "But, just so you know, things have a way of not going as planned. I'm living proof."

Kerri raised a finger. "Me, too."

Great. Not exactly a comfort. But at least the subject was dropped. And she didn't give it much thought as they all pitched in to carry the bride-to-be's loot to her car.

After Caitlin reassured her and Kerri that the Dalton brothers would unload the car once she drove her sister home, Holly followed Kerri back inside to help her clean up.

She needed to keep busy. Each day that passed felt like she was living on borrowed time at her real job. Sooner or later, the other shoe would drop and take her job with it. And she couldn't blame them.

Arms laded with empty dishes, she headed for the kitchen, only after making sure the pregnant woman was directing the servers on breaking down the buffet table and not lifting a finger herself.

Happy to be useful, Holly pushed through the swinging door into the kitchen and walked right into…

Doctor Hottie.

Despite the shock of literally running into the doctor where she never expected, she was proud the squeak that escaped her lips was a small one. And somehow, between the two of them, they managed to keep her armful from falling to the floor.

"Whoa, I got you," he said, steadying them.

What she got, was her heart fluttering and pulse pounding in her ears. "Sorry. I-I didn't know anyone was in here."

He grabbed half her load and carried them to the sink. "I'd just finished taking out Connor's stitches."

"Oh." She set her stack next to his, then turned to face him. "I didn't know he had any, or that you made house calls."

That caused all kinds of crazy, hot thoughts to rush through her head all at once. And the blood to rush to her face. *Dammit.*

Smile tugging his lips, the handsome man stepped close to brush a strand of hair off her cheek. "He did, and I do…when my patients are too stubborn to come to me."

Something in his tone told her he had been prepared to seek her out about her arm. Good thing she'd run into him at the office building then, because the last thing she needed was to be alone with the tempting, sexy man.

Like now.

She tried to draw in a breath, but her thudding heart was stuck in her throat, blocking passage.

"How's your arm?" He was dressed casual today in jeans and a white T-shirt.

She wondered if he looked as good without his clothes. "What?"

"Your arm? How is it?" he asked, again.

She tilted her head back. "Fine." Truth was, she couldn't really feel her arm, or the rest of her body for that matter, with him standing so close. Everything was sort of foggy, even her brain; although, thoughts of the kiss they'd shared when he'd last examined her arm were quite vivid at the moment.

His gaze dropped to her lips and heated. Yeah, he remembered the kiss, too. She opened her mouth, managing to drag some air into her starved lungs, her mind suddenly screaming for her to step back to break the chemistry. But it was no use. Her body was not cooperating with her brain.

"Very…fine."

His voice came out so husky her good parts quivered.

But what was lethal was the delicious scruff covering his jaw, something she'd only seen a few times on him, always when he was off work for a day or so. And his eyes. Fathomless clear, blue pools, searching deep for her secrets, yet giving nothing away of himself.

"Like that kiss we shared. We haven't talked about it. Maybe we should."

"The kiss was…fine," she repeated, and his eyes narrowed. *Better than fine. Incredible times infinity divided by amazing with a cherry on top.* He just stared at her. "Okay," she admitted, sagging against the sink. "So, we both know it was great. But I'm not looking for a…a…thing. Or for a guy like you."

"Like me," he said slowly, as if the words didn't make sense.

She nodded, regaining a little bit of her thought process. "Look, Jace, we've been through this. You know I'm not going to be in Texas much longer, so while I'm here, it's probably best if I stay away from fun."

"So…no fun."

"Yeah. It's for the best."

"Yeah."

He stepped closer, and since there was no place to go, she found herself sandwiched between the sink and his delectably hard body. He set his hands on her hips, where they squeezed before they slid up her sides, over her ribs, to her arms and her shoulders. By the time his touch trailed up her throat and cupped her face, her body was singing an 'Ode To Jace' tune.

She swallowed. "What are you doing?"

"Testing a theory."

His husky whisper sent a shiver down her spine, and she knew what he was doing. He was building the anticipation, heating her from the inside out. And it was working, dammit. She didn't want this attraction, and yet, her body strained a little closer.

"What theory?"

His gaze met hers and held. "That the chemistry we felt before wasn't a fluke. Do you still think it doesn't exist?" he asked softly.

"I…" She swallowed hard.

He quirked a brow. "Say it, Holly."

"Fine. So, maybe we have a little chemistry," she admitted. "But it doesn't—"

He dipped down and nibbled her lower lip, then stroked and teased her with his tongue until a helpless murmur of arousal rumbled up her throat, and she fisted his T-shirt.

His eyes were heavy-lidded when he drew back. "Nothing little about that."

Warm hands stroked her back through the thin material of her sundress, while he slowly lowered his head, giving her plenty of time to push away. She didn't. Oh, she should have, but lust had taken over and zapped the smart from her brain.

Their gazes held until his lips brushed hers, all warm and firm and so damn fine her lashes swept down involuntarily, savoring the feel.

With a deep, male sound, he threaded his hands through her hair, tilted her head, then kissed her, lightly at first, then urgent and hungry, devouring her strength until all her bones melted. By the time he broke the kiss, her legs were like rubber, and breathing was erratic as if she'd just skied the expert slope. Uphill.

"I don't think that helped," she said between breaths, releasing his shirt to smooth out the wrinkles.

He stared at her through those gorgeous, heavy-lidded eyes and stood there looking dangerously alluring and hotter than any man, cowboy, or doctor had a right to, all while slowly shaking his head.

"It's okay. I'm not looking for a relationship with you either," he said quietly. "I've got enough on my plate between my mom and sister and work. Plus, with me leaving next spring to join Doctors Without Borders, I'd be crazy to bring a woman into my life now."

He was joining DWB? Her heart cracked open a little more for the seemingly selfless man. This made him much more dangerous. Good thing they weren't looking to hook up.

"So, we're in agreement," she said with relief. Too bad she didn't feel any. Why didn't she feel relieved? Neither of them wanted a…a…thing. So, where in the world was her relief?

He nodded, dropping his gaze to her mouth. "Thanks for understanding."

"And thank you, too," she whispered, then bit her lower lip in an attempt to stop it from trembling.

He groaned, and the sound was so hungry and male, her toes curled.

"Holly."

"I know. This is nuts." She tried to move away, but whacked the side of a cupboard.

"Easy there." He cupped her head in his palm.

They stared at each other, and without her permission, her dang hands made their way up his chest and over his shoulders. Before she knew it, her fingers were playing with his hair. His dark, silky, sexy hair.

Another low sound emanated from his throat before he pulled her back to him. Then they were kissing again, and her hands skimmed down his muscles and explored the ones up his back while he did some examining of his own.

"Hey, Doc, I forgot to mention this new craving I…oh, sorry."

Connor's voice penetrated her fogged brain. She stilled, then tried to pull away, but Jace held tight, brushing a kiss near her ear.

"Damn, you're dangerous," he whispered before slowly drawing back, making sure she was steady before he released her.

"No need to stop. My apologies again, for interrupting." The tall cowboy held up his hands while shaking his head before his gaze settled on Jace. "We can talk about *Kerri's* cravings on the mini round up later. Thanks for volunteering to help today, by the way. I appreciate you rushing over, like Tanner, to fill in. This flu that's going around knocked out three of my men."

Holly stepped forward, resisting the urge to glance sideways at the enigmatic man who seemed to wear many hats—doctor, guardsman, cowboy/cattle wrangler, best kisser in the world—and focused instead, on his friend. "I hear ya," she said. "Two of my uncle's workers have it, leaving me shorthanded with no choice but to leave Donny in charge today."

It had been a hectic week, but she'd been happy to keep busy. She was so over this not knowing when she could leave, and if she still had her job.

"Donny?"

A grimace rippled across the rancher's face, bringing her mind back to the conversation. She laughed. "Yeah, so, if you'll excuse me. Now that I'm done helping your wife clean up, I'd better go check to see if the shop is still standing, and not painted in ice cream."

With a quick nod to both men, she hurried from the kitchen, grabbed her camera from the other room, and double-checked with Kerri to make sure the woman didn't need any more assistance.

"No, I'm good." The pretty mother-to-be smiled as she pulled her in for a hug. "Thank you so much for your help. I can't wait to see the photos."

Holly drew back and returned her grin. "You're more than welcome, and me, too," she said, before fleeing the ranch.

Her rush had everything to do with Donny and the state of The Creamery, and nothing to do with needing to put space between her lips and the good doctor.

Nothing at all.

Not a bit.

Nadda.

As far as Holly was concerned, that was her story, and she was sticking to it.

The next day, Jace was at his family's ranch, trying to cross as many jobs off his list as the day would allow. Every Monday, he stuck a blank piece of paper on the fridge for his mother and sister to jot down things that he needed to tackle on the weekend. With his day unexpectedly devoted to the McCalls yesterday, that left him less than twenty-four hours to accomplish forty-eight hours' worth of work.

A quick call to Jesse and Tanner had produced two volunteers to lend a hand. He appreciated the help, especially knowing their time was limited. Jesse had his grandfather's ranch to run, and Tanner was stretched between helping Kade at Shadow Rock, Connor at Wild Creek, and volunteering as a firefighter. And yet, both men had agreed without question.

Walking into the barn, Jace had his own question. What was going on between his sister and Jesse? The air was so thick with tension, he needed a scalpel to slice a path inside.

"So…" He eyed the two who stood at opposite ends of a stall, staring each other down.

Forget the scalpel. Lacey's glare was like twin lasers. Damn, he wouldn't want to be on the receiving end, and did not want to know the cause. Noting Jesse's thin lips and clamped jaw, he was betting the lean cowboy was doing his damnedest to keep from saying something Lacey would make him regret.

Jace stepped toward his sister. "You here to help, too?"

"Yeah, like you'd let me lift anything heavier than a feather," she scoffed.

He shrugged. "Maybe two." Damn right he wouldn't let her lift anything. She was recovering from a broken back. When she didn't even crack a smile at his joke, he blew out a breath. "Lace, I know you want to get back to how things were before, but you can't."

"That's bullshit, Jace. But you're right. I can't. Not with you, and the *warden*, monitoring my every move."

The reason for the tension just became clear. He glanced at the still quiet man. Jesse, no doubt, wouldn't let her help. Probably told her to leave. A smile twitched his lips. Nobody told Lacey to do anything.

"Don't worry. I'm leaving. There's way too much testosterone in here. I can't breathe," she said, brushing past him to head for the door as Tanner rolled up on his Harley.

"Hey, Lacey," the firefighting guardsman greeted, strolling inside.

"Hey, Tanner," she grumbled. "You're just in time for the penis party, but I think Jesse's got you beat. He's the biggest prick I know."

This had the firefighter howling as he neared. "Man, Jesse, what in the hell did you say to her now?"

Jace wasn't sure he wanted to know.

Chapter Five

No one could rub Jace's sister the wrong way faster than the quiet cowboy.

Jesse ripped the hat off his head and waved it at the now vacant doorway. "I told her to go back in the house. We didn't need her to muck anything out."

Tanner stilled. "Shit."

"Yeah." The dark-eyed cowboy nodded as he jammed the hat back on his head and got back to distributing hay around the stall.

"I don't know what's scarier." The green-eyed cowboy rubbed his jaw and stared thoughtfully at Jesse. "You telling Lacey Turner to go back to the house, or her wanting to help while still recovering." He dropped his hand and faked a shiver. "They're both bad."

Jace stepped forward and cupped the Jesse's shoulder. "Well, I appreciate you looking out for my sister. I know she can be a handful."

The man's lips twitched. "Easier to rope a tornado."

"Amen." Tanner nodded.

For the next several hours, the three of them took care of every chore on the list, including tending to the handful of livestock his mother had insisting on keeping around because they were his father's favorites. Jesse had just finished shoeing one of the horses as he and Tanner hung up tools from fixing the south end of the corral.

"Well, I'd say we earned a beer or two," he stated.

The lean cowboy held his hands up. "If it involves going into the house, I'll pass."

"Yeah, me, too," the laidback guardsman agreed. "We've only been back from deployment a few months. I'd rather avoid another war zone."

Jace glanced at the house and nodded. "Chances are, Lacey's in her room sulking."

"That makes her even more dangerous."

"Yeah." Jesse nodded. "I think it's best we leave."

"And fast."

He laughed as he shook their hands. "Thanks for the help. I appreciate it."

"No problem, Doc. We take care of our own."

"Yep. You've done it for others in your platoon plenty of times," Jesse reminded. "We'll catch you later."

The setting sun cast a warm glow over the ranch as Jace walked back to the house after the taillights of a pickup and Harley disappeared down the drive. It had been a long day, and he was dogged tired, but pleased they'd accomplished everything on the list. He'd rest easier knowing there were a few less things for his sister to try to tackle around the ranch. She was making great progress, and he intended to keep it that way.

Short of hiring a babysitter for the headstrong woman, he had no choice but to make sure there was nothing strenuous to do. He knew it was pissing her off, but he didn't rightfully care. His sister's health was more important to him than her pride.

"There you are," his mother said, wiping her hands on her blue flowered apron when he entered the cozy three bedroom ranch. "I was about to come out and fetch you boys…" She glanced around him. "Where are Jesse and Tanner? I made chicken and dumplings."

"They went home." He grinned. "I guess that means I get extra."

She returned his grin. "You never could pass up seconds on my chicken."

"No, ma'am." He washed up, then joined her at the table. "Where's Lacey?"

"Right here." His sister waltzed into the room, her gait only slightly stiff, thanks to her rehab. "I was just making sure it was pri—I mean, jerk-free."

"Lacey! I don't know what has gotten into you lately," their mother scolded. "That's no way for a lady to talk."

"Sorry, Momma, but that man just gets me so mad sometimes." She blew out a breath, then said grace before she ripped a biscuit in half and shook it at him. "And I don't know what you said to him, Jace, but Jesse seems to think he can boss me around."

Doing his best to hold back the grin that threatened, he studied his younger sister. It was rather interesting to see the unruffable woman all in a huff. "I haven't said a thing, but if you keep trying to do too much too soon, I just may hire him to work around the ranch every day, just to keep an eye on you."

Her biscuit hit the table, crumbs bouncing in the air as she glared at him. "Don't you dare, Jace Raylon Turner."

He shrugged, buttering his own biscuit, watching the golden goodness melt into the nooks and crannies. "I won't." He lifted his gaze and stared straight at her. "As long as you stick to your restrictions."

After a moment's hesitation, and a few heated emotions rippling across her face, she finally nodded. "Fine. I'll be a good girl and do only what my physical therapist allows."

"Good." He nodded, then dug into his chicken, happy to drop the subject and its underlying tension. His life was hectic enough. Last thing he wanted was stress at home.

"Okay, now that we have that settled," his mother said, slicing into a dumpling. "I have a question of my own."

"Oh?" His sister frowned, shoulders stiff as she braced herself.

His mother laughed. "Not for you. This is for your brother."

"Me?" His chicken-laden fork paused in mid-air as he narrowed his gaze on the brown-haired, blue-eyed woman. With the exception of a few wrinkles and smattering of gray strands, you'd never know she was pushing sixty. "What's wrong? Are you not feeling well?"

"Oh, I'm fine," she insisted, placing a hand on his arm. "It's *you* I'm wondering about, hun."

"Me?" he repeated. "I'm good, too."

"That's just it. You're smiling, and happy for a change. It's been so long to see you like this. I'd love to know who she is."

He stiffened, and glanced at his sister whose mouth split into a big grin.

"Yeah, come to think of it, Jace, you have been grinning a lot lately." Lacey pointed her fork at him. "Does this have anything to do with Holly and her desserts?"

"Holly?" His mother's eyes lit up. "Arthur's niece that was so sweet to leave her home in Colorado to run his shop while he recuperates?"

"Yeah, her," Lacey replied before he could. "I heard he kissed her yesterday over at the McCalls."

"Well now. That is good news."

His mother and sister continued to hold a conversation about him while he sat at the table with them. Stomach clenched tighter than his jaw, he barely moved as the women discussed his love life as if it were an episode from a sappy soap opera.

"Do you think it's serious?"

"I don't know. Maybe Jace could answer that." Lacey transferred an amused gaze to him. "So, how about it, bro? Is it serious between you and Holly?"

His mind tried to play catch up. The two women were tossing out questions right and left. He blinked and set down his fork. "It was just a kiss."

Okay, technically their *second*, incredible kiss. But that was not something he'd share. Instead, he shrugged and picked up his fork in an attempt to throw them off the scent. His mom was forever suggesting 'nice' woman to him, hinting at wanting grandchildren. Last thing he needed was for her to sink her teeth into something that wasn't there.

"Yeah, a pretty hot kiss, from what I heard."

His sister was not helping with her silly grin still present.

"Kind of like the one you shared with Jesse," he said, and watched the smile disappear from her face, exactly as he'd expected. What he hadn't counted on was the blush that rose into her cheeks.

Lacey Jane Turner never blushed. Ever.

Interesting. He'd apparently hit on the source of the tension that had been ongoing between his sister and his friend the past few weeks. Somewhere in that time frame, the two must've kissed.

Oh, man. God bless, Jesse. He was going to have his hands full, if the poor guy decided to pursue the obvious chemistry.

"I like Holly," his mother continued.

She completely ignored the elephant in the room—Lacey's blush. Which meant his mother already knew about his sister and Jesse. Maybe he *was* working too damn much. That would explain how he'd missed the fact those two had kissed.

"She's always so personable when we stop in at The Creamery, isn't she, Lacey?"

"Yes, and don't forget beautiful. What I wouldn't give to be able to wear my hair short and flirty like her. It would just make my face look fat. But not her, she's stunning with those pretty green eyes."

"Yes, I noticed them, too. They kind of grab you and take hold, don't they?" his mother asked no one in particular.

The two women ate and talked, while he sat there with a knot in his chest the size of Texas. Which made no sense. So, he kissed a pretty woman and enjoyed it. Big deal. It's not like they had something hot and heavy going on.

"I think it's great that you're seeing her, Jace. You deserve to be happy."

He cleared his throat. "I'm not seeing her, Mom."

"Well, you should. It's not right to go around kissing girls you're not seeing."

Lacey tried to mask her snicker behind a napkin pressed to her mouth.

She failed.

"I like Holly," he finally said, feeling a measure of relief at having admitted it out loud. "But it's not worth pursuing with me joining DWB in the spring, and her about to go back to Colorado as soon as her uncle's doctor clears him to work."

"Then you shouldn't be kissing her. It's not nice to lead a woman on." A deep frown grooved her forehead. "I thought your Dad and I raised you better."

He blew out a long breath. "Yes, ma'am."

His mother's delicious meal suddenly tasted like cardboard as guilt flooded his gut. It was a sad day when he didn't clean a plate of his mother's cooking. But, today was going to be one of those days.

"Then, either keep your lips to yourself, hun, or start seeing the woman."

"Yes, ma'am," he repeated.

Too bad both options were near impossible.

Holly was excited to make it to Wednesday without a work crisis. Work—at The Creamery—was going smooth. The fact that Donny only had a few hours on Monday evening was probably part of the reason, but she tried not to blame summer work mishaps on just one employee, despite the poor kid being the only commonality.

This week had been family crisis free, too. Her uncle was back to making *remarkable progress*, as his PT had put it, and Doctor Turner had just confirmed.

She currently sat off to the side on the couch in the handsome man's office, while her mom and Uncle Arthur occupied the chairs in front of his desk. As he asked her uncle some routine questions, her pulse hiccupped, listening to his deep, sexy tone, and her lips tingled, remembering the feel of his when he'd kissed her stupid in Kerri's kitchen last Saturday.

All damn week, she'd tried hard not to give his kisses much thought. She failed. Every time she thought her lust was under control, memories of their two embraces fluttered through her mind. Making her hot. And bothered. Like now.

Dammit.

She shifted in her seat, and drew in a slow, deep breath. He turned to her, and with his face averted from her family, he met her gaze with a knowing, heated one of his own. *Oh boy. Not helping.* Not helping her rein in her out of control feelings. This was all new. She'd never had crazy, uncontrollable emotions before. Not even with her ex-boyfriend of two years.

Uncharted territory, that's what it was, and apparently Jace felt the same, if the frown and slight shake of his head were any indication. A second later, a neutral expression claimed his features before he returned his attention back to his patient.

The muffled sound of Queen filled the air. Holly quickly swiped her purse off the floor. Never more thrilled for an interrupting phone call, she fished out her cell, then excused herself and hurried from the room to answer the call from her brother.

"Hey, what's up, Zach?" she asked, walking into what she assumed was a break room, happy to find the small kitchenette and round table and chairs deserted.

"Hi, how's Uncle Arthur?"

The million dollar question. "His PT said—"

"His what?"

"His physical therapist."

"Oh."

"He said he was making remarkable progress."

"Well that's good, right?"

She nodded as if Zach could see. "Yeah."

"Does that mean you'll be coming home soon?"

For some strange reason, her stomach sank. Which was stupid. Why in the world would her body have that reaction when she'd been chomping at the bit to head back to Colorado? Refusing to dissect the possible answer, she leaned against the wall and shrugged. "I think so. We're at his regular doctor's now. We're hoping Jace…I mean, Doctor Turner can shed some light."

"Oh, good."

After several beats of silence, Holly got the impression there was more to the unexpected call than a polite inquiry of their uncle's health.

"So, what's up? Are you okay?"

She hated that her younger brother was in another state all by himself, even though they all knew it couldn't be helped.

"Yeah, sort of."

Now her heart stopped. "Define *sort of*."

"I'm good, but, well, my professor asked if I'd be interested in going to Japan to teach English to children over the holiday break in December."

"Oh, Zach, that's wonderful!" She straightened from the wall. The very reason the smart, compassionate man was majoring in Asian Studies was to see some of the eastern world, experience other cultures, and teach English to the locals. "It's exactly what you want to do with your major."

She was secretly envious of her brother's bright future, and guilty because of the envy, having resigned herself to helping her mother and brother financially, and living vicariously through Zach.

"Yeah, thanks. There's just one problem…" His voice trailed off.

Holly stilled, her pulse increasing to warp speed. "What?"

"Money."

Why was that always the problem? She sighed and slumped into a chair, mentally calculating what was left in her meager checking account after paying rent and utilities on the apartment she shared with him, even though she wasn't there. "How much?"

"I qualify for two grants, but I still need to come up with over a thousand dollars."

A weight settled across her chest. "By when?"

"The beginning of November."

Damn. That was two weeks away. Her heart sank, but she didn't want her brother to know. "Okay. I'll see what I could do."

"How, Holly? You're already stretched thin, and I hated to even tell you."

"No. Don't ever feel that way, Zach. You know I'm always here for you."

"Of course I know, but who's there for you, Holly? It seems all this family ever does is turn to you for help. I'm so sorry."

Between the tears suddenly blurring her vision, and her hot, tight throat, she wasn't able to answer for a few seconds. "Don't be sorry, hun. I'm good. Honest." Now, if she could just hit the lottery, she'd be even better. "So, don't you go worrying about the money. I'll come up with it somehow. You just fill out whatever paperwork you need to get the ball rolling."

"Okay." Her brother sighed in her ear. "Thanks, Hol. I love you."

"Love you, too, Zach." She disconnected, then dropped her head on her arms folded on the table. Her family may not be rich in cash, but it sure was rich in love, and she'd be damned if she didn't figure a way to help her brother out. No way was Zach going to miss out on this opportunity.

Even if she had to sell her camera.

Her stomach hollowed at the thought, but if it came down to it, she would sell her prized possession.

"Everything okay?"

Jace's deep voice sent a warm quiver to all her good parts, and the warm hand he set on her back kick-started her pulse as he sat next to her at the table.

"Yeah. Thanks." She lifted her head, then sucked in a breath at the concern darkening his eyes.

No man had ever looked at her with real concern, unless they wanted something in return. For the life of her, she couldn't figure out what he had to gain by showing her compassion in the middle of his office lunchroom.

"Bad news?" he asked, wiping her wet cheek with his thumb.

She cleared her throat and shook her head. "No. Not really. My brother was asked to study abroad over the holiday break."

A genuine smile crossed his lips. "That's wonderful. What's he studying?"

"Asian Studies. He's going to Japan to teach English to children. If I can come up with the money." She blew out a breath, and threw back her shoulders. "Not *if*. When. I will. I've got two whole weeks to think of something. No way is Zach going to miss out on this opportunity."

Between medical bills and his business, she knew her uncle was strapped, so asking him wasn't even a consideration. Holly felt guilty enough accepting a paycheck from him every week, even if she got him to agree to only pay her minimum wage. And if she hadn't needed it to pay for her apartment back home in order to keep a roof over Zach's head, then she never would've taken a cent. The wonderful man was already letting her live rent free in one of the small cottages he owned by the gulf.

"If anyone can come up with a solution, you can," Jace said, admiration and a few unrecognizable emotions skittering through his incredible, clear, blue eyes. "You're something else, you know that?"

A warmth she'd never known, or expected, heated her from within, drying her throat, so much so she couldn't speak. Only shake her head. No one outside of her family had ever said that to her before, and she had no idea what to do with the emotions jumbled inside.

"Well, you are…" His voice trailed off as his face drew nearer.

Chapter Six

Holly's heart pounded so loud in her ears she thought her head might fall clean off. Which would suck, because then she wouldn't get the eminent kiss.

"Holly? Where'd you go?"

Jace's lips barely brushed hers when her mother's call came from the hallway.

They simultaneously broke apart and stood.

"I'm back here, Mom."

She cleared her throat and wiped the remaining wetness from her face, just as her mother breezed in, appearing a lot closer to her forty-nine years than the sixty she'd seemed that morning. Less stress looked good on her mom.

"You ready to go?" Holly resisted the urge to fan her face. Lordy, she hoped she didn't look as flushed as she felt.

"Oh, you found her, Doctor Turner." Her mother smiled, handing Holly the purse she'd left in Jace's office. "Yeah, we're ready. Your uncle's in the waiting room." She frowned. "Who was on the phone?"

"Zach," she replied, dropping an arm around her mother's shoulder as she led the woman from the room, glancing back to smile her good-bye to the quiet doctor. "Wait until I tell you the good news."

It was half-past five, and Holly had just finished eating the comfort food supper she'd made of grilled cheese, with a macaroni and cheese chaser, when a knock sounded at her door. Not expecting company, she stacked her dishes in the dishwasher, then answered on the third knock, surprised to find her redheaded friend on the doorstep, face a bit taut with anxiety.

"Hi, Holly," Shayla greeted, fretful smile twitching her lips. "Sorry to drop in unannounced, but, do you mind if I come in?"

"Of course not. Please do." She stood aside, her mind racing with thoughts as to what could be causing the apprehension tidal-waving off the bride-to-be. "Why don't we sit down and you can tell me what's going on?"

Shayla nodded as she stopped pacing and sat…on the coffee table.

Holly bit back a grin and motioned toward the couch. "Maybe you'd be more comfortable here."

"Oh, for crying out loud, I'm turning into a damn ninny." Blushing, she joined her on the sofa. "Between this wedding and the baby, I have no brain left. Thank God, my fiancé is a genius, because he makes up what I'm lacking right now. Take this dilemma with the photographer. It was Kevin who suggested you."

"Me? For what?"

"The photographer we hired for our wedding has a family emergency and can't make it on Saturday. Kevin suggested I ask you, and I think it's absolutely brilliant."

Holly blinked, her pulse picking up speed. "You want me to photograph your wedding?"

That was huge. Super huge. She could hardly believe her friend would entrust her to capture such a momentous occasion.

"Yes. Please say you will." Shayla squeezed her arm. "We're freaking in love with the ones you emailed to me of the shower last weekend. Why in the world aren't you doing this for a living?"

"But this is so important," she replied, ignoring the last question. Mainly, because her answer sucked. Saying her father wouldn't support any type of artistic training would no doubt resurrect bad memories for both of them. Better to stick to ignoring.

Her friend squeezed her arm again. "That's why I'm asking you."

For the second time that day, Holly's throat burned with unshed tears because a friend believed in her.

"So…what do you say?" Shayla's anxious blue gaze held tight. "Will you photograph my wedding?"

She opened her mouth, but nothing came out, so she cleared her throat and tried again. "Of course…?"

Her friend's squeal was probably heard in the next county, and Holly thought maybe she'd suffered a ruptured ear drum. But she'd never been so damn happy and wholeheartedly returned the tight squeeze the little redheaded, pregnant, bride-to-be laid on her.

"Thank you, Holly. Thank you so much. You're a life saver," Shayla claimed, then pulled out a check with a whole lot of zeroes at the end. Enough zeroes to take care of Zach's bill, and then some.

She drew back and shook her head. "Oh no. That's way too much. I'll do it for free."

"Hell-to-the-no, woman." Her friend frowned, setting the check on the coffee table before she stood. "You're photographing my wedding, therefore, you'll get paid for photographing my wedding. Kevin wanted me to give you a bonus for saving our ass, but as I suspected, you're giving me trouble just accepting the going rate."

Holy shit.

That was the going rate to photograph a wedding? Maybe Shayla was right. Maybe she *was* in the wrong business. And her friend was right about another thing. She was definitely going to give her trouble accepting the check, no matter how badly her brother needed the money.

She rose to her feet and cupped Shayla's shoulder. "You're a friend, and friends don't charge friends."

"You're wrong, Holly." The woman touched her arm and hit her with an earnest stare. "They don't charge them for cooking dinner, or babysitting. This is different. Please say you'll photograph my wedding, because if you won't let me pay you, I'll have to try to find someone who will."

Several emotions sweep through her at once, but finally her desire to help her friend overrode everything else. She blew out a breath and nodded. "Okay. I'll do it. But not for a penny more than is on that check, which I won't be cashing until you hold the photographs and give me your approval."

"Deal."

She was pulled in for another tight hug, which, she again, returned wholeheartedly before she scooped out two heaping bowls of Death-by-Chocolate ice cream she had in the freezer to celebrate.

As they discussed possible shots and poses, Holly couldn't stop grinning at the excitement and adrenaline sparking inside. She was going to need more supplies than she'd brought with her to produce a wedding album that was going to rock Mr. and Mrs. Kevin Dalton's world.

After he locked up the office that night, Jace headed to his car with one thing on his mind. Cheering up Holly.

One look into her distraught gaze that afternoon had cracked something open in his chest. He never wanted to see that emotion clouding her beautiful green eyes again. Ever. And when determination had replaced her distress, and she vowed to help her brother no matter what, he fell a little bit more for the woman whose selflessness touched his guarded heart. All day, his mind kept returning to their conversation in his lunchroom, and he couldn't let it go.

So, instead of heading home, he turned right and drove to The Creamery. Maybe, together, they could somehow brainstorm a solution to her problem. He already knew better than to offer her the money. She would never take it, and he understood. It was more a matter of principle than pride. Just one of many things he was beginning to realize they had in common.

After he parked his car, he walked up the steps to the boardwalk, not convinced the surge of blood rushing through his veins was solely due to the exertion. Donny waved to him from the window on his approach.

"Hi, Doctor Turner. If you're looking for Holly. She isn't here."

The blood rush came to a halt. "Oh. Okay. Thanks, Donny," he said, glancing down the street to her cottage. Her car was in the driveway. He turned back to the grinning kid and ordered two smoothie specials. A good brainstorming staple.

Two Key Lime Swirls in hand, he strode to her cottage and knocked on the door, noting the return of the mysterious blood rushing in his veins thing, which he decided to label the *Holly Affect*.

When his knocks went unanswered, he glanced around. She had to be somewhere between her house and the shop. He checked behind her little blue cottage and found her small yard and patio both empty. So, he headed down a trail that led to the beach…and stopped dead.

Chapter Seven

The *Holly Effect* clicked into turbo charged at the sight of the namesake lounging on the beach with her dark hair blowing haphazardly around her delicate face, shoes kicked off, jeans rolled up, and setting sun bathing her in a breathtaking, bronze glow.

The sight of her grabbed Jace by the throat, and for a moment, he couldn't breathe. This 'fighting the chemistry' thing was hard as hell.

What a coincidence. So was he.

He glanced down at his bulging crotch and smirked. When the hell had he become so easy?

When the green-eyed temptation had waltzed into his office.

No, that wasn't quite right. It wasn't exactly her looks that caught and held his attention, even though she was beautiful as hell. It'd been her heart. The little things he noted about the woman. How she listened to Mrs. Avery, a retired school teacher and local dance instructor, talk about her cats when the octogenarian came in for cream for her 'babies,' or how she delivered the cream when the older woman couldn't come in. The way she hired unqualified workers and kept them on, not because they did a great job, but because they sucked at it, but tried with all their might.

She rewarded heart with heart, and damn, if that didn't get to his.

Big time.

"Hey," she said, holding up a hand to shield her eyes from the setting sun, as she glanced up at him with her gorgeous, open gaze. “What are you? A mind reader now?”

Unsure of her meaning, all he could do was stare down at her and play stupid. Apparently, he was good at that, and amusing, because she laughed.

“Mind reader?” he asked as he handed her a smoothie before sitting next to her in the warm sand.

She laughed again, and the sound caused a strange, warm and fuzzy reaction in his chest.

“Yes, this,” she said, holding up the cup. “I was just sitting here, enjoying the sunset, thinking, man, I could sure go for a smoothie right now. And there you were, smoothie in hand.”

Her genuine smile was contagious.

“Glad I could be of assistance.”

“You always seem to have just what I need. Or say just what I need to hear.”

“Funny, I was thinking the same about you.”

He watched her mouth close around her straw, fascinated by the way her cheeks indented as she sucked, the motion way too erotic for his already aroused state to ignore. White, hot heat shot straight to his groin. He swallowed and forced his gaze back to her eyes.

She blinked, but her gaze remained dark and heated, and he fought to remember why he was there. He dragged air into his lungs, and salt from the ocean clung to the back of his throat.

Her brother. Tuition.

Right.

It took him a moment to find his thread of thought, and tamp down his desire. “I stopped by The Creamery, and when you weren't there, I bought two smoothies and tracked you down.”

“Why?”

Unsure if she was asking about the drinks, or the tracking, he decided to give an answer that resolved both questions. "To help you brainstorm a solution to your brother's tuition."

She stopped drinking, and lowered her cup, a thousand watt smile spreading across her face. "It's already solved. A half-hour ago, Shayla hired me to photograph her wedding."

"That's terrific," he said, clinking his cup off hers. "To problems solved."

They sat drinking in silence for a few minutes, and every now and then she'd glance at him and frown.

"What?" he asked, twisting to face her.

"It's just…you said you went to The Creamery?"

He finished his smoothie and nodded. "Yeah. I thought I'd try to help you brainstorm, but it turns out, you've already found a solution."

Her gaze rounded. "You really stopped by to help me?"

The very fact she found this hard to believe resonated something deep inside him. "Surely, your friends in Colorado have helped you before?"

When she set her drink down and shook her head, but remained silent, his heart clutched a little in his chest, understanding all she didn't say. There was nothing he could do to stop his hand from reaching out to cup her face. He wanted to do more than touch her physically. The overwhelming need to touch her heart, made no sense all, yet, all the damn sense in the world.

He skimmed his thumb across her lower lip. "I think you need new friends."

"Agreed," she whispered, gaze huge, and so open, he ached. "Is that what we are, Jace? Friends?"

"Hell yeah," he replied, still touching her face, figuring it was probably him that had shifted closer. "That okay with you?"

Holding his gaze, she shocked the hell out of him when she planted a kiss to his palm. "Very. But we seem to have a problem with the no-touching thing."

"I know," he said, before capturing her lips with his, intending to keep the kiss gentle, and slow, but her hands went to his chest, her warmth radiating through the material of his shirt, changing his mind, and the kiss, in a flash.

Of heat.

Body flaming, he groaned as the need to consume shook through him. Then her hands were suddenly under his shirt somehow, skimming down his chest, tracing his abs, driving him mad.

"Holly," he croaked, his voice tight and hoarse as he grabbed her hands in an attempt to remain clothed, which was a good thing, considering they were in public.

She dropped her forehead to his shoulder and drew in ragged breaths, the air cooling his chest where she'd popped the buttons. "I'm sorry. My mind knows this is a bad idea, but the rest of me doesn't care."

A strangled noise of agreement rumbled up his throat.

"Jace?"

"Yeah?" He drew back to see her face illuminated by the sunset.

She reached up and traced his jaw with her thumb. "My mind is starting to not care either."

"Good. Mine, too."

Then they were kissing again, this time with more gusto, probably because they'd just mutually tossed caution to the ocean breeze. He traced her lip with his tongue, loving the way she moaned and opened up for him, sliding her tongue against his, testing his control. She did it again, adding her touch to the mix, her hands gliding up into his hair.

With a groan, he pushed her back into the sand, covering her fully, and at the contact of their bodies, she let out the sexiest damn sound and wiggled beneath him.

She had great wiggle.

He ran a hand down her side, then under her shirt, finding her skin soft and hot. So damn hot. She trembled and held him tighter, and he needed more. Much more.

Breaking the kiss, he drew in air as he brushed his lips down her jaw, his body thrilling as she clutched his back and arched up. He nuzzled her neck and skimmed his hand over her ribs to cup her breast, brushing his thumb over her nipple poking through the lace.

She gasped, so he did it again, capturing her mouth for a deep, soulful kiss. He knew they were out of control, but couldn't stop the wildfire consuming him from the inside out.

"Ahem."

They both stilled at the sound of a throat clearing, and Jace cursed his stupidity for putting them both in such a foolish position. He drew back slightly, being sure to shield Holly's body from view as he righted her clothes.

"Maybe you should take this elsewhere."

Ah, hell. He recognized the woman's voice. And so he should. He'd gone to school with Jordan McCall.

"Okay, Sheriff," he said, staring down into Holly's face.

Her eyes rounded, and he braced himself for a chewing out, but instead, she brought a hand up, slapped it over her mouth, and laughed.

Taking it as a good sign, he smiled as he rolled off her and got them to their feet. Once again, Holly surprised him. She had every right to be pissed at him, and yet, she took it in her stride.

"Sorry, Jordan," she said.

In another surprising, possessive move, she slipped an arm around his waist.

He liked it. A lot.

Holly patted his chest. "One minute we were talking, the next we were out of control."

The sheriff smiled. "I completely understand. Been there. Done that. Cole makes me nuts. Sorry to interrupt you, but I just wanted to save you from…overexposure. And a fine."

"We appreciate it, Sheriff," he said, still cursing himself for even having this conversation.

He was an educated man. A platoon leader. A damn doctor. With responsibilities. Not some hormonal adolescent riding the wave of sexual adventure. Although, he glanced down at the woman pressing her delectable curves into his side. Holly seemed to flip that switch every damn time she touched him.

There was no such thing as control with her around.

"No worries. I—" The sheriff paused as her radio crackled to life with dispatch informing her of a two car accident on the interstate, with medical attention needed. She glanced at Jace. "I hate to ask you, but can you come? I already know the fire department and paramedics are with my deputy at a house fire."

He released Holly and nodded. “Of course. I’m right behind you.” He turned to the woman at his side and reached for her hand. “Sorry. I have to go.”

“I know. It’s okay,” she reassured, her smile barely visible in the dwindling light. “I can find my way home. I’ll be fine.”

But would he?

The more he was around the sweet, giving woman, the more he faced that very question.

The morning of Shayla’s wedding brought smiles for several reasons. Holly was beyond happy for her friend, and basked in the love flowing from everyone in the large bedroom at the Dalton ranch where the bride-to-be and her attendants gathered to get ready.

Hustle and excitement brought a magical feel to the air, wrought with tangible electricity. Her body hummed with a wonderful energy as she snapped photo after photo, pausing to pose the bride every now and then, marveling at how breathtaking Shayla was in her white gown full of lace and delicate appliqué that captured the woman’s strong, yet feminine personality. Jen, Kerri, and Jordan, her bridesmaids, were beautiful in their green satin dresses that hit the knee with lace and appliqué, while Caitlin, the maid of honor, wore a dress similar to the bridesmaids, except in a deeper shade rimmed in silver.

Then there was Amelia. The cute little flower girl couldn’t stop twirling, giggling at the white, gauzy material swirling around her legs, while she chanted, “Mommy, Daddy.” A pretty, green satin ribbon circled her waist, and little daisies were placed in her hair that was piled on her head like the rest of the women in the bridal party.

Holly captured the sweetheart's animated features as she twisted and giggled. For a whole hour, she clicked away, documenting the morning with photos, some posed, some candid, and all with a smile on her face.

She couldn't stop smiling.

Adrenaline rushed through her veins as she studied the scene, the women, the room with a critical eye, searching for the best angles and lighting, determined to capture gasp-worthy photos for her friend.

"You are rockin' behind that camera, Holly." Jordan approached with a grin. "I think maybe Shayla would love a few photos with you in them. How about you show me which button to push, and I'll make it happen?"

The bride-to-be stepped closer to grab her hand. "Yes, I definitely want a few with you in them."

Holly spent the next five minutes on the other side of the camera, laughing and joking and smiling in front of the lens.

She'd never felt more relaxed and alive at the same time and vowed, then and there, that no matter what happened with her job in Colorado, she was definitely going to look into taking some classes on professional photography.

"Oh, Shayla. You look absolutely stunning," Mrs. McCall said, walking into the room. "Kevin is going to faint."

Everyone laughed. The thought of the brilliant, easy-going, cowboy computer programmer reaching the sort of stress level needed to faint, made Holly smile. The man was gorgeous, and after having photographed the groom and groomsmen in his room an hour ago, she knew the black-haired, blue-eyed man's good looks were only going to compliment Shayla's stunning presence.

"They're ready for you," the older woman said, brushing a tear from her face. "What do you say we go line up and get you married?"

Shayla nodded, blinking back her own tears as her smile widened. "Yes, it's time I made an honest man of Kevin."

They were all still chuckling as they walked through the house on their way to the gazebo Kade, Connor, and Tanner had built especially for the occasion. Holly had already photographed the beautiful structure all decorated in white satin and roses, representing hope and pure love of the start of a new life together. The setting was stunning, and she marveled at the incredible job Brandi had done of designing and arranging the rows of chairs, runners, and flowers for family and friends to witness the union. Even more incredible was the way the designer had temporarily transformed the new barn, being built for shelter animals, into an elegant, yet casual venue for the reception to follow.

When she'd first arrived that morning, Holly started with the empty structures, capturing the promise they held with sunlight and shadows representing the ups and downs of married life the couple would face. She'd witnessed marriages fail, and marriages that shined. Judging by the way Kevin and Shayla treated each other the past few months, she had a good feeling about the couple and the staying power of their relationship.

She had a good feeling about someone else, too.

The gorgeous doctor, dressed in a black suit and tie, sitting with his mother and sister in one of the rows.

Every time his gaze strayed to hers, he'd smile, and heat zinged to her center, waking all her good parts.

The man was too distracting. Way too distracting. That's why she'd made a point of giving him a wide berth the past two days. Two days since she'd nearly gotten indecent with him on the beach.

She still couldn't believe she'd lost control like that, like a school girl with her first real crush. Man, she was such an idiot, and yet, she just couldn't bring herself to regret the beach. It had felt too great. Too right.

Too stupid.

You live in Colorado, she silently reminded as she lifted the camera to her face and started photographing candid shots of the guests while waiting for the music to start. Okay, so she had a few extra shots of Jace in there. Couldn't be helped. He sat near the end, and she needed a few pictures of the beautifully decorated aisle.

And him.

Dammit.

Twisting around, she kept her back to him and faced the house just as the music began to play. Blood rushed through her veins once again, and creativity took over.

She slipped easily into photographer mode. Shayla and Kevin trusted her, and *paid* her, to record their special day, and she intended to earn every last cent, and enjoy herself in the process.

For the first time, in a very long time, she was happy.

The bride and groom wore matching, blissful grins as the reverend pronounced them man and wife.

There hadn't been many a dry eye when Caitlin walked Shayla down the aisle and gave her sister away to the grinning groom. Tears continued when the couple recited their own vows. Jace had to admit, he'd been impressed with Kevin's poetic, heartfelt prose. The laid-back cowboy had always been full of surprises. No reason his wedding shouldn't have a few, too.

Instead of choosing a simple waltz for their first dance as man and wife, the couple busted a groove to Maroon Five that had Mrs. Avery on her feet, clapping, along with half the guests. Then the bridal party joined in, bringing everyone to their feet, camera's flashing, people laughing, and he was most impressed with Kade.

"Shit." Tanner stopped next to him and pointed. "I had no damn idea Top had rhythm. Did you?"

He shook his head and smiled. "Hell no."

Although, he'd never really been anywhere with Kade to see him dance, except for military Dining Outs, and then he'd preferred the slow songs.

Like him.

"Me either," Jesse said from his other side.

"I didn't even know the first sergeant knew there was music beyond Johnny Cash," Tanner observed as they watched the bridal party having fun on the dance floor.

The music changed to another popular dance song, and the guests began to take the floor. Tanner wasted no time escorting a pretty blonde to join the fun, but Jace and Jesse remained where they were, happy to watch the crowd.

Well, maybe Jesse watched them. Jace's gaze strayed to Holly, as it had the whole damn day. The woman captivated him. Her exuberance and energy, and beautiful smile that had not left her lips once that day, all gripped him and held tight.

She wore a pretty, flouncy, light green sundress that skimmed her knees just above a pair of killer brown cowboy boots with fancy swirls of light green. Her hair was piled on her head with little pieces left loose to brush her temple and neck, exactly where his lips longed to be. She looked amazing, and he actually ached at the sight of her. Again, it wasn't just to touch her physically, he wanted to reach inside and touch her soul as she had done to him.

Jace didn't understand what set this woman apart from the others, and there had been others, some who were pretty, and nice, and sweet, and wanted to settle down. But there was always something missing. A connection.

Not the case with Holly.

She got past his defenses, breathed life into his dormant heart. And he was damned if he knew what the hell to do about it.

The timing couldn't have been worse, and yet…

She turned then, and their gazes met and held above her camera. A second later, she lowered the device and smiled. Something actually fluttered in his chest.

"You should ask her to dance," Jesse said.

He wanted to. Real bad. But, for the past two days, he'd been careful to steer clear of the tempting woman.

"No. Too dangerous. Her nearness sucks the smart from my brain and turns me into Doctor Stupid."

The cowboy smirked and lifted his beer in a toast. "I heard that."

"You have the same issue with my sister, don't you?"

"Yep." Bottle raised again. "And I'm not all that smart to begin with."

Jace laughed. "Bullshit."

Sergeant Jesse Briscoe had the best damn hands in his unit. He could turn a tin can, bobby pin, and chewing gum into an internet hot spot. The man was an electronics genius, and a damn good friend.

"If I was so smart, I'd be going over there to ask Lacey to dance, instead of leaving, now, wouldn't I?"

He watched the man set his empty bottle down, then head for their newly wedded friends. After a kiss to the bride's cheek, and shake of the groom's hand, Jesse did exactly what he'd said. He left.

Jace slid his gaze to his sister, not at all surprised to find her watching the sergeant's retreating form, disappointment dulling her eyes.

Until she caught him watching her.

Amazing how quickly she wiped all traces of emotion from her face. Had him wondering what his sister was hiding. And why.

"Since you were just rolling around with Holly in the sand the other night, it seems a little strange to find you standing clear across the room from her." Jordan appeared at his side, her tan sheriff's uniform ditched for a pretty green bridesmaid dress. "Aren't you going to ask her to dance?"

Chapter Eight

Jace smirked. "You're the second person to ask me that."

"How did you answer the first time?"

Not sure he wanted to repeat himself, he shrugged.

A grin tugged the sheriff's lips. "Look, if it's a matter of stupidity, we're all guilty of that, Jace."

He glanced sideways at the beautiful woman who always appeared put together and a pillar of strength for the county. "You? Stupid? Sorry, not buying it, Jordan." He smiled.

"Aw, you're sweet, Doc, but very misguided." She gave him a quick hug then released him, holding his gaze. "The heart plays no favorites with stupidity. This one time, when I was still in college, I hadn't seen Cole in years, we weren't dating but I was missing him so bad, I hopped on a plane and flew to Houston to track him down. I didn't tell him, or anyone. I thought it'd be really cool to surprise him." She shook her head and let out a sad laugh. "Stupid."

Remembering how the two had been so close growing up and both upset when she'd moved to the west coast before she'd graduated high school, he couldn't imagine Cole turning Jordan away after being apart for a few years. "Why was that stupid?"

"Because, as I was crossing the busy street to get to him on the other side, a pretty blonde came out of the building and rushed into his arms."

He blew out a breath. "Bess." His heart squeezed for the young, eager, Jordan who, no doubt, had been crushed to see the love of her life with his first wife.

She nodded. "Yeah. So, I gathered what was left of my shattered heart, and snuck back to California to lick my wounds."

Her gaze sought and rested on Cole who was dancing with his mother.

"It all worked out in the end," he felt compelled to say after a few beats of silence.

"Actually…" She turned to him and grinned. "It had worked out then, too."

"I don't follow."

"It may have been stupid not to call, or to have waited so long, but if I had never gone, then I would've *always* pined for Cole, and never would've given my first husband a chance. And even though Eric's death still haunts me, I don't regret that relationship one bit, Jace. Not one. Damn. Bit. You get what I'm saying?"

He nodded, his own chest a bit tight. "That not taking a chance is more stupid."

"Exactly." She smiled. "Life is too short. No one knows what fate has in store. Hell, if someone had told me that day in Houston that I would actually marry Cole someday, I would've thought they were insane."

Jace laughed. "Yeah, and yet, you did."

The couple had reunited a few years ago at the McCalls' fortieth anniversary. It hadn't exactly gone smoothly. Cole had been too riddled with guilt over Bess' death, and Jace remembered treating the head of the multibillion dollar company for some drunken mishaps that first year. Then Cole had quit cold turkey and retreated into a shell. A year later, Jordan had visited, and managed to pull his friend from that dark pit.

Well…more like dragged his sorry ass into the light.

"Yes. I did," she said, gaze growing soft as she smiled at her approaching husband.

He watched Cole cup his wife's face and kiss her with such tender care, eyesight was not required to see the emotion flowing between the couple. It was felt, like a spark in the air. Even though it may have taken them a few tries, the couple had finally gotten it right.

"My wife talking about me again, Jace?" Cole smiled, tucking the woman against his chest.

Jordan winked at him. "Always. It's your fault for always being on my mind, honey."

A big smile spread across the man's face. "Ditto."

Suddenly feeling like a third wheel, Jace excused himself before his indecision over Holly became a topic for discussion again. He had no idea what fate had in store for him, or if the green-eyed photographer laughing at something Tanner leaned in to say was part of the picture. He only knew he liked looking at her, liked touching her, liked being with her. She made him feel good. Happy. And it had been so long since he'd been happy.

"Hi," she said a little breathless, as he stopped in front of her. "Having a good time?"

A Lady Antebellum ballad began to play. "I'll tell you in a minute," he replied, lifting the camera from around her neck and handing it to Tanner before leading her to the dance floor and pulling her in close. Feeling her sigh as she melted against him, he closed his eyes and tightened his hold. "*Now* I'm having a good time. I've wanted to hold you all damn day."

"Funny. I've wanted you, too," she said against his neck, causing a shiver to race down his spine. "But, I had pictures to take, and still do."

He increased his hold, not ready to release her. "After this song."

"Not yet." She nodded, and her hair tickled his jaw.

Then she was nuzzling his neck, and inhaling, sending another round of shivers down his spin.

"Mmm…you smell good. You always smell good."

Heat rose to the surface as her soft curves moved seductively against him. He swallowed back a curse and closed his eyes, which turned out to be a bad idea. Very bad idea. Worse idea in history. It amplified the sensations, and he was rock hard in seconds.

"You're killing me," he said against her ear, his voice rough with the need pulsing through his body.

"Good, because thanks to you, I can't feel my legs." She chuckled, holding him tight. "Don't think I'll be much good at taking pictures flat on my back."

His heart rocked hard in his chest at the image she just created. He'd love to get her flat on her back, again. "I rather like you in that position. You felt incredible on the beach the other evening."

A muffled moan met his ears as she burrowed against him and trembled. "You do not play fair, Doctor Turner."

The bold woman was one to talk. She nipped his earlobe, then soothed it with her tongue. He sucked in a breath and swallowed back a curse, but before he could retaliate, the song ended, and she pushed out of arms.

"If you'll excuse me, I'd better get back to work."

Before she moved too far, he grabbed her hand and tugged until her back hit his chest. "We're not done," he warned quietly against her ear, then released her after he felt a tremor run down her body.

If he hadn't been certain before, he was certain now. The no-touching rule officially bit the dust.

He wanted her.

She wanted him.

Tonight, it wasn't about family obligations, work, or even future endeavors. No. Tonight, it was strictly about what Holly needed and wanted, and what he needed and wanted.

And right now, he wanted Holly.

Bad.

Holly had never wanted any man so bad in her life. Jace made her nuts. Made her see stars. Stole her breath, and they'd only shared a few hot kisses. Being in his arms was becoming her new favorite place to be, but every time she tried to seek him out at the reception, someone had asked her to take their picture for Shayla and Kevin's wedding album. And since that's what the couple was paying her for, she'd had to push her needs and wants aside and do her job.

For the better part of the day, she'd been happy to do just that, but after spending one damn song in the doctor's strong arms, snuggling against his hot, hard body, Holly wanted to stow away her camera and concentrate on touching Jace.

And licking him.

Too bad he'd had to take his mother and sister home before she had a chance to make any sort of plans with him. She'd waited around, stalling as she snapped photos long after the bride and groom had left on their honeymoon.

Pathetic.

"Maybe it's for the best," she told her reflection in the mirror above the sink in the bathroom at her cottage later that night. She stared at her flushed cheeks, and the eagerness lighting her eyes. *Yeah, pathetic.* "You need to get a grip." Her sigh fogged the mirror as she began to remove the pins from her hair. She'd been home twenty-six minutes, unloaded the dishwasher and swept the floors, but her body still hummed with a pent up energy Jace had sparked.

Maybe she'd upload the photos and start weeding out the keepers. Not like she had anything else to do. Or anyone.

A knock sounded at her door.

Her hands stilled as her gaze collided with her reflection's. A flush deepened in her cheeks and her heart skipped a beat. Was the good doctor making a house call?

No. Probably Donny needing help with a research paper again. The last time he'd brought over his notes, she couldn't decipher history dates due to the incredible caricature of his professor he'd sketched in the side margins.

Holly hurried to answer by the third knock, nearly falling on her face when she tripped over the boots she'd kicked off a good twenty-five minutes ago.

Wobbling on one foot, she answered the door while rubbing her throbbing toe, then stilled at the sight of Jace, minus the jacket and tie, leaning against the frame, gaze dark and hungry…and determined.

Her pulse tumbled, knocking the breath from her lungs. Damn, he looked good enough to eat. And she was suddenly starved. For him.

"I know I shouldn't be here. But…" His sexy voice trailed off, leaving the ball in her court as he leaned closer and lifted a hand to brush a strand of her half-pinned up, half half-fallen down hair from her face.

He was so close, she could feel his warm breath on her temple. She'd never been so aware, so tuned to a man's body. Or her own.

She shifted closer and placed her hands on his chest, marveling at the heat radiating under her palms. The man was on fire, and her knees shook at the intensity. “I, ah, think you and I both know this…*thing* between us is too big to ignore anymore.”

“It’s time we stopped trying.”

She nodded. “I agree.” Her fingers curled around the material of his shirt, and she tugged him inside. “Now works for me.”

“Works for me, too,” he said into her mouth as he shoved his hand in her hair and finally kissed her.

Someone managed to shut the door; she knew this because she was suddenly pressed against it, heat zinging through her body as his lined up perfectly with hers. She moaned, and he wasted no time putting her opened mouth to good use.

There was a difference in his kiss and touch. No longer tentative, or slight, it was as if he knew what he wanted…her.

He demanded and took and gave with a zest that left her breathless and begging for more. Normally, she would’ve been shocked at her utter lack of control. Not tonight. Not now. Not with the hot, hard, and hungry man rocking into her while his tongue slipped in and out of her mouth with matching rhythm.

The feel of his warm hands on her body, gliding over her waist and hips, then back up, skimming her breasts as if he needed to touch every inch, had his name tumbling from her lips in a heated breath. She needed to touch him, too, and trailed her hands all over his magnificent body. He felt so damn good, her insides quivered.

A corner of his mouth quirked as he drew back slightly to drag in a breath. “I wanted to do that for three days now.”

"Then what took you so long?"

His lips were back on her body, kissing a path down her jaw to the curve of her neck, making it damn hard to concentrate on conversation. Then there were his hands. Warm and big, gliding up and down her sides, sending tiny shivers all over her body.

"Stupidity." He slid her a sheepish grin. "I foolishly thought this chemistry could be ignored."

"Me, too," she admitted, unbuttoning his shirt while holding his gaze. "Guess that's stupidity times two." She pushed the opened shirt over his broad shoulders and watched it fall to the floor.

"Not anymore."

She stared at him. With his hair all tousled, thanks to her roaming hands, and heat darkening his eyes to a delicious deep blue, she kept forgetting he was a doctor, and she didn't date doctors anymore. Until now.

Until Jace.

He got past her defenses with his easy charm, and genuine, caring heart. The man made her feel good about herself, made her want to be a better person. A truthful person.

"I haven't had sex in almost a year. Not since I caught my boyfriend with my best friend."

A dark emotion skittered across his face, replaced by something warm and unwavering. He ran his knuckles lightly across her cheek. "He was an idiot."

"I keep telling myself I don't miss it. That I don't need it."

His eyes were dark. Very dark. "Bet I can change your mind," he stated, and before she knew it, he picked her up and carried her across her small living room straight through her open bedroom door.

Her heart knocked her ribs several times before settling back in her chest. *Oh boy.* Her whole body just sparked to life.

He set her on the mattress, then sat next to her, those broad shoulders of his blocking out most of the light as he leaned in. "I'm going to take good care of you, Holly."

Her ribs took another pounding from her out-of-control heartbeats. "Good."

"Very good," he said, shifting closer, then closer still. "Do you know why it's going to be good?"

"Because we have chemistry."

"Exactly."

Jace reached for her, his hands closing around her upper arms before he slowly pulled her up against him. He was close. So deliciously close she only had to lean forward just a hair and their lips would touch. But she held back. Eager to see what he had planned.

He stared at her mouth, his eyes heavy and heated, and she shook with an anticipation that raced to all her neglected good parts. The easy strength with which he held her against his hard chest had butterflies fluttering in her stomach. He was still gazing at her mouth, his jaw flexing as if it was an effort to hold back.

"Do you feel that, Holly?"

Hell yeah.

She was feeling so much it was hard to form words. She nodded, sliding her hands over his broad shoulders to cup the back of his head. Pressed up against his rock hard body, she let out a small, needy sound as desire shot to parts south. Deep south.

"Feels good, Jace," she murmured in his ear.

"Very good," he said again, before he leaned in, pressing her down until her back hit the mattress.

Towering over her, he looked magnificent, all sinewy and ripped, and hungry. Those fathomless eyes stared into hers, letting anticipation drum between them, driving her a little bit insane before he finally bent to kiss her.

Eager, and just as hungry, she opened her mouth for him, sliding her tongue against his, thrilling at the deep groan that rumbled in his chest. He tightened his hands on her, and her body responded to the need she felt in his touch by making room for him between her legs and arching up to rock against him.

"You're killing me," he said as they broke for air.

She smiled. "Sorry."

He let out a chuckle and set his forehead to hers. "Liar."

The feel of him all pressed up against her was too much, and she couldn't stop her hips from undulating. He muttered a curse and pressed back with his impressive erection.

She cupped his face, loving the feel of stubble against her palm. "You drive me crazy, too."

Holly watched her thumb skim over his lower lip, trying not to panic at what she'd just revealed. It'd been a while since she'd felt so moved. In fact, she hadn't really ever experienced this foundation rocking, earth slipping movement before.

He whispered her name in a low, husky tone that had her insides quaking and told her he was feeling just as unnerved. That made her feel better. She wasn't alone in this uncharted, emotional frenzy.

Slowly, he lowered his head and kissed her again. Long and deep and wet. The sensual kiss shut down what little brain power she had left. And...*damn*, he tasted hot and bold and intensely male.

"I want more than a kiss," he murmured. "I want everything, Holly. So, if you don't want to give it, then you need to tell me."

"No way I'm stopping…" she whispered, pulling his head back down. "Take what you want. I'm all yours, Jace."

Chapter Nine

At this, Jace let out the sexiest damn groan and did as Holly said. His lips devoured, taking what he wanted without apology. Their embrace went from aroused to frenzied and wild; their hands touched everywhere as they took turns on top, her dress tangling around her legs. She kissed and licked and panted, enjoying the journey south, down his six-pack abs. Then, suddenly, she was flat on her back with her wrists clamped in his hand and pressed high above her head.

She moaned. Couldn't help it. He covered her completely with his entire weight. Crazy with need, she wrapped her legs around him, bringing him in tighter against her.

"Damn, Holly," he murmured against her mouth, then pressed hot, open-mouth kisses down her throat.

She gasped when he bit the special spot behind her ear, then turned her head to give him better access.

Yeah. There. Her eyes fluttered shut, so overwhelmed with sensations. The air changed. Amped up. It was crazy. Insane. Delicious.

"Jace…"

"Tell me."

"I want you."

The instant the words were out, he shot off the bed, shucked the rest of his clothes, then was back, leaning over her, barely giving her a glimpse of the glorious splendor that, moments ago, had pressed heavily between her legs. Jace slipped the straps of her sundress down her arms, tugging until the material slid to her waist. When he discovered her braless, he stilled and sucked in a breath.

"Were you at the wedding all day without…?"

"Yes." She smiled, running her hand up his sleek chest.

Holly watched as he muttered something and closed his eyes as if fighting to hold onto his control. A second later, he gazed at her, eyes dark and heated as he dipped down, kissing the curve of her neck, nipping her collarbone, then kissing the side of a breast, before gently sucking on the tip. The feel, the motion, was so wonderful, so perfect, she arched up, pushing more into his mouth.

An incoherent sound rushed from her lips, full of need and hunger, which would have horrified her if she'd been alone in the frenzy. But for once, she wasn't alone. Given the low, sexy sound that rumbled through his chest, conveying hunger and impatience, he felt it, too.

Still teasing her nipples with his wicked tongue, he pushed her dress down and over her hips, bending so he could reach to yank it off. Never one to remain idle, she slid her hands down his sides and around to cup his fine ass. He made that rumble sound again and thrust against her before releasing her breast to draw back and glance down at the only piece of material separating them.

Her blue lace, hi cut bikini panties.

"Ah, hell…you had them on all day, too?" he asked, his smoldering gaze slamming into her.

She cupped his face and grinned. "Yep. So…what are you going to do about them?"

His chest was warm and deliciously hard against her as he lowered his lips to within an inch of hers.

"Guess you'll just have to wait and see."

His eyes were lit with heat and humor, and she had the sudden urge to taste him. As if reading her mind, he brushed his curved mouth over her, kissing her slow and languid, building a fire from all that simmered inside. When he finally lifted his head, he stared down with so much heat and intensity, she shivered.

"I can't wait to be inside you."

His words liquefied her bones, and she grabbed his ass again and rocked up, her good parts pulsing in anticipation.

"Please tell me that's going to be soon."

"In a hurry are we?"

Jace chuckled and pushed with his thigh to open her legs farther, then settled in as if he'd been made for the spot. Holding her gaze, he slid his fingers between her thighs.

When he stroked, she cried out, so damn ready and needy it was almost pathetic. But it was too good. His touch was so delicious, so perfect, a switch tripped somewhere deep inside, intensifying the feel so much she nearly lost it on the second stroke. Then he lowered his head and kissed her nipple, rasping his tongue over the tip, and then again, while her breath hitched in her suddenly dry throat.

"Whatever you do, please don't stop," she panted, her body amass with sensations.

"Yes, ma'am," he said against her flesh, sliding his finger under the lace and tugging the bikini panties down as he kissed a path over her ribs, her belly button, and hip. Lifting his head, he watched as he removed the final barrier, sucking in a breath at all he'd revealed. "So perfect."

"Jace—"

He palmed her thighs and nudged until he wedged his shoulders between her legs and took in the view.

Her heart was pounding ruthless in her chest. "I need…"

What? She didn't know for sure.

He did.

The deliciously intuitive man leaned forward and lapped at her, ripping silly, needy little mewing sounds from her throat, but she didn't care. She sank her fingers into his hair and held on for the ride. Rocking into him, she cried out when he added his fingers.

Damn. He was good. *So good.*

She trembled, straining, every muscle taut and seeking release as she clutched him with shocking desperation, so close to the brink. It'd never felt like this. Like she needed him to bring her to climax more than she needed to breathe. In tuned to her needs, he held her at the edge for a beat before sending her over with a long, sure stroke.

Fast and intense, her orgasm burst through with merciless speed. Jace cradled her, bringing her down slow as she shuddered against him. She would've asked if he'd gotten the number of the bus that just plowed her down, but that would require talking, and she still needed a moment to find her voice.

He lifted his head and smiled at her. "You taste fantastic."

His words sparked heat low in her belly, shocking her that she could recover so soon. He drew back and fished a condom out of his pants on the floor. The play of light on his muscles and ridges had her itching to reach for her camera to capture his magnificence, but when her gaze got to his powerful thighs and…*damn*…all the glory in between, she lost coherent thought. A knowing grin curved his lips, and with efficient, precise movements, he was sheathed and looming over her within a few seconds.

Jace ran a hand up her legs, and let out an appreciative groan when he slipped a finger easily inside her fold. "So wet." Then he brushed his lips over her belly, her breasts, to her mouth, and kissed her as he settled between her legs and entered her.

Instinctively, Holly angled her hips, giving him further entry, and when he pushed all the way in, their twin gasps of pleasure echoed throughout the quiet cottage. Need hitting her fast and fierce again, she automatically rocked into him when he began to move, a delicious heat consuming her every pore. She'd never felt so good, so filled, so whole.

"Damn…you feel good," he whispered, his big hands cupping her head as he deepened the kiss, sliding his tongue inside her mouth with the same delicious pace and intensity as his thrusts inside her body.

She was done. Her body hummed. Fingers clutched, gripping his hips as she teetered on the blissful edge again, and when she came, he followed her over with her name on his lips.

Unsure how long she laid there, eyes closed, dragging in air, holding the spent man to her equally spent body. He seemed to be in no hurry to go. Warm breath hit her skin in spurts as he nuzzled her throat, still rocking his hips, prolonging their pleasure.

Was there such a thing as satisfaction overload? With Jace, she was beginning to think it was possible. He just took her out of herself, on some incredible pleasure trip, and she was still gasping for breath like she'd just skied across the whole damn state of Colorado.

"You okay?" he asked, rolling onto his side, lifting his weight off her.

She blinked at him. "Not sure. Can't really feel my legs."

His grin, loaded with pride, was lopsided as he traced a line from her bottom lip, down her throat to a breast. "I'll take that as a yes."

"You would." She snickered, smacking his shoulder. "What the hell just happened, Jace?"

He shrugged, gaze suddenly serious. "No idea. My mind sort of blanked once I sank inside you."

"Well, Doc…" She cleared her throat, while running a hand down his hot, damp chest. "I may need more while I'm in town. How about it? Think you can fill that prescription?"

Heat entered his gaze, and his erection thicken against her leg as he brushed her nipple back and forth with his thumb.

"Yes, ma'am. As a matter of fact, I think I can fill that for you right now."

Two days later, Holly stood with Tanner at the rental shack where they returned their boards and paddles after meeting him for an enjoyable afternoon at the lake. She was still wearing the smile brought on by what she labeled as her *orgasmic weekend* with Jace. Turned out, the good doctor was an expert with more than just his hands. The things he'd done, and she'd done, Saturday night and all day Sunday, left her sore and so damn satiated she was good for several weeks.

Although, if he was to show up on her doorstep again, she wouldn't turn him away.

After slipping her shorts and tank top on over her bikini, she joined Tanner at a picnic table, eager to tear into the lunch they'd bought at a refreshment stand. She was a little surprised they were still open. Summer officially ended almost four weeks ago. Heck, back in Colorado, a few places kicked off their ski season in mid-October. Sitting in her bathing suit in eighty degree weather at this time of the year wasn't exactly the norm for her.

Then again, she'd been acting out of the norm a little lately. Images of a certain sexy doctor leaning over her all naked and hard flashed through her mind.

"All right, I'll bite. What gives?" her friend asked halfway through his burger. "You've been wearing that grin ever since you showed up this morning."

She shrugged. "Nothing. I'm just happy, that's all."

"Ahuh." His gaze narrowed. "There are happy grins, and there are *happy* grins. And you, my friend, have the latter."

Not one to kiss and tell, she just smiled before returning to her own burger.

His low chuckle filled the air. "I'll have to give props to Jace for putting that smile on your face. It's nice to see you happy and relaxed."

She was certainly that. Lord knew she was still riding the satiated train from the weekend. "It's nice to feel it," she said, reaching for her bottle of water without admitting his friend had been the cause.

"Hol, if you were any more relaxed, you'd be asleep." He snickered, then leaned closer. "So, does that mean you two are a couple now?"

She probably shouldn't have gasped while drinking her water. Coughing and sputtering, she pounded on her chest in an attempt to clear her airway. "No," she croaked, wiping the wetness from her face. "We're just friends."

"Having sex."

She lifted a shoulder. "What's wrong with that?"

"Nothing." He shook his head and sat back. "I think it's great. I just never pegged you for the casual type."

She wasn't. Not normally.

"It can't really be anything more than that, can it? Not with me leaving soon, and Jace planning to join DWB next year."

"No reason you can't keep it going from a distance."

She swallowed another bite of her burger, then narrowed her gaze on the persistent man. "Is there a reason you're pushing for us to be a couple?"

"I happen to think you two are good for each other. You have a hell of a lot in common. You're both hard-working over-achievers who put family first."

She shrugged. "Lots of those around."

"Not really. But, even so, you're good for Jace. He hasn't had it easy, not since his father contracted HIV after a blood transfusion from a car accident when we were kids."

Holly stilled at that piece of news. Jace's desire to join Doctors Without Borders made even more sense now. She'd read somewhere how the humanitarian organization treated people stricken with the disease in third world countries. It was no stretch at all imagining Jace driven to help.

"After that, life was a constant struggle for the Turners," her friend continued.

She wished she could get him to stop. Hit the mute button. Put her fingers in her ears. Personal information about her temporary lover was not a top priority for Holly. In fact, she'd specifically resisted asking Jace anything personal during their romp the past weekend. Much easier to keep things casual when you didn't know each other's life story. Easier to leave when you didn't get personal.

"Then his father died of complications from pneumonia a few years ago while we were deployed."

Her heart squeezed. "How horrible."

Ah, hell. Now her heart was involved.

Tanner nodded. "I was with him when he got the call. I'll never forget the look on his face, Hol. The guilt and torment and loss…" He slowly shook his head. "He hasn't been the same since. It's almost as if he'd stopped living for himself…until lately. Until you. Some of that old spark is back. He's not so stuffy."

She didn't know what to say to that, so she decided it was best to say nothing.

"And you definitely seem a lot happier."

An orgasmic weekend will do that.

Trying desperately to come up with a subject change, she was saved by the bell when Tanner received a call about a structure fire. He shot to his feet, tossed his garbage in the nearby trash, then came back to the table and frowned down at her.

"Sorry. Got to go," he said. "See you same time next week?"

"Yep."

But she hoped not. She needed to be back in Colorado…because she was beginning to not want to leave.

And that was bad. Very bad.

As she watched her friend hop on his Harley and head to the fire, she couldn't help but relate. This thing between her and Jace could get out of control, real fast. And damn if she wasn't drawn to it. To him.

And that was bad. Very bad.

Every time Jace tried to see Holly that week, life got in the way. His crazy, hectic life. There were times, he hated to admit, that he needed a break. His spine hadn't been the only thing to melt in the beauty's arms. The world, and all its expectations and problems seemed to disappear when he was buried deep inside her warmth. And he liked it. A lot.

After spending twenty-six straight hours of pleasure with the woman, he thought he'd have to drag his ass home, but instead, he'd left her cottage, five nights ago, feeling alive. Rejuvenated. Ready to take on the world.

Now…not so much.

He blew out a breath and headed down the corridor in his office building, trying to decide how to spend what was left of his lunch hour. Crashed out on the couch in his office, or eating in the hospital cafeteria next door.

Question was, what did his body need more? Sleep? Or sustenance?

Holly.

A smile tugged his lips. She was sustenance, release, and relaxation all wrapped in a soft, curvy, caring package. He could get used to that kind of lunch hour. Which, if he caught up on his sleep and was in his right mind, he'd know wasn't smart.

His curved lips slowly straightened, and he was back to being tired, overworked, stretched thin, dealing with his family, his patients, not to mention Doctor Parker's, too, after the man had suffered a gallbladder attack early Monday morning. The older physician ended up in the hospital to have it removed the next day, and Jace ended up fitting in some of his colleague's patients.

His plans to make the most of whatever time Holly had left in Harland County had gone up in smoke. He just hoped she'd be around another week, and that he'd free up some time, because he already knew this weekend was shot. He had drill with the National

Guard, and by the time he left the armory and got back to the ranch, he'd have just enough daylight to tackle one, maybe two chores off the growing list on the fridge—a list still noting chores he'd neglected last weekend due to the wedding…and his twenty-six hour rendezvous with Holly.

"Hi, Doctor Turner."

He stopped and turned toward the vaguely familiar female voice to find Holly's mother smiling as she walked toward him in a pair of jeans and pumpkin-colored shirt that brought out the brown in her eyes. And left him to conclude Holly had inherited her eye color from the father she rarely discussed.

"Hello, Mrs. Phillips. How are you?"

"I'm good," she replied, appearing a lot less stressed without the constant frown and tense jaw he'd gotten used to seeing. "Just here to drop some paperwork off for my brother's ortho doctor."

"I take it Arthur's doing well. No more falls?"

A hand devoid of jewelry and polished tips settled over her chest. "Oh my goodness, no. He learned his lesson."

"I'm glad."

"And I'm glad I ran into you." She glanced around the deserted hall and stepped closer. "I wanted to talk to you about my daughter's boyfriend, Tanner Hathaway. I understand you know him?"

Chapter Ten

Jace stilled, rooted to the spot by an invisible spear that felt as if it lanced his chest and impaled him to the tiled floor. All he could manage was a nod.

"Holly insists he's not her boyfriend, but she spends a lot of time with him, and…well, they're young, and probably having sex, so I was just wondering what kind of man he is." Mrs. Phillips drew in a breath, the frown and tenseness around her mouth returning.

He could feel them creasing his own face as his stomach knotted with some unknown emotion.

"My brother said the poor boy was dropped off at his uncle's ranch when he was eight," she stated. "Arthur doesn't know anything about Tanner's parents, but said the uncle was a…well, I'd rather not repeat. It wasn't a nice word."

Because there were no nice words to describe Bart Hathaway. He'd been a mean drunk who beat Tanner every chance he got, until his friend had grown several inches the summer he'd turned sixteen and punched back.

"I'm sorry, I don't normally meddle, but Holly was hurt pretty bad from her last boyfriend, and I just don't want to see her get hurt again. You understand?"

He nodded, not really understanding anything past the fact his insides felt as if he'd swallowed a box of nails, after chewing on glass, then washing it all down with acid.

Realizing the concerned mother was waiting for a reply, he brought what he hoped passed as an honest smile to his face. “Tanner is a good friend, firefighter, guardsman, cowboy, you name it. He’s always the first to volunteer whenever you need a hand.”

And a commitment-phobe who never stayed with one woman for very long.

Not something Holly’s mother would be all that happy to know. Not something *he* was all that happy about if his friend was actually *seeing* the same woman he was…*seeing*.

“Well, thank you for being frank with me, Doctor Turner.” The woman smiled, relief evident in the softening of her forehead and mouth. “I’ll let you get back to work. It was nice talking to you.”

With that, the woman turned and walked away, disappearing around the corner while he stood there staring at the hall…suddenly feeling just as empty and hollow.

And no longer hungry.

Jace turned and headed back to his office, calling himself all kind of names for even considering that Holly was sleeping with Tanner. Then calling himself another round of names for thinking she wasn’t.

Too keyed to sleep now, he strode past his office to the lunch room where he grabbed a banana from the bowl of fruit on the table. It was none of his business. Why was he letting it bother him? He didn’t want a relationship. His life was way too hectic and crazy for him to saddle on any woman. Hell, he didn’t have time for one. Even one as giving, great smelling, great tasting as Holly Phillips.

So, why was she constantly on his mind?

The phone in his pocket rang, saving him from a round of soul searching he was not ready to do. He glanced down at the caller ID and groaned.

Lacey.

He wasn't sure he was up to dealing with his ornery, bored sister, either. Setting his uneaten banana back on the table, he answered the call.

"Hey, Jace," she said, sounding stressed, not bored. "Sorry to call you at work, but I didn't know what else to do."

Her tone and words shot his blood pressure into orbit. "What's wrong, Lacey? Did you fall? Are you okay?"

"I'm fine. It's not me. It's Beckham."

Her damn horse?

The one she'd named after some "gorgeous soccer player," as she'd put it. He squeezed the bridge of his nose and blew out a breath, undecided whether to strangle her for scaring the shit out of him, or cheer because she hadn't reinjured her spine.

"He got loose and took off in the south pasture. I told you he needed daily exercise. He's going stir crazy since I haven't ridden him in weeks."

"I thought you were going to talk to Jesse or Kade and let them handle your horse until your doctor gave you the all clear."

"Kade has enough on his plate with the rescues."

True. Last Jace had heard, his friend was sheltering a malnourished mare and her foal.

He waited a beat for his sister to continue; when she didn't, he spoke up. "And Jesse?"

Another beat.

"Lace?"

"What?"

"Did you ask Jesse to exercise Beckham?"

"No. You know I don't like when he's around. He's too damn bossy."

Jace closed his eyes and shook his head. "He's also good with spirited horses. Swallow your damn pride, or get over whatever issue it is you have with the guy and ask him for help."

"Hell no."

He tried another tactic. "I thought you cared about Beckham."

"That's low, bro."

"Look, I'm sorry," he said, softening his tone. He knew the past few months had been rough on his independent sibling. "I love you, Lacey, and I know you're used to doing everything yourself. But, right now, you need to accept help until you're fully healed. It's only temporary. Okay?" More silence. "Lace?"

"Okay. You're a sneaky SOB, you know that?"

He smiled as relief filtered through his body. "Runs in the family."

This got him a chuckle. "Touché."

"So, you'll call Jesse?"

"No. I was hoping you'd come home during your lunch break."

He glanced at the clock on the wall and grimaced. "Sorry, sis. I have an ear infection, UTI, and stitch removal all in fifteen minutes."

"Well…hell."

Welcome to my world, he thought with a sad smile.

"Guess that leaves Mom and I."

He sat up. "Hell no." Damn, stubborn woman. "I'll call Connor."

"Tried. No good. Kerri said he was in Loughton Springs delivering a bull for this weekend's annual fall rodeo."

Damn. "I'll try Tanner." He was ashamed to admit he was a little reluctant to talk to his friend. Which was stupid. He had no right to feel…whatever the hell rippled through his gut at the thought of Tanner and Holly together.

"Tried him, too. He's not answering. I figured he might be with some chick."

That unknown emotion rippled through his gut. Again.

"Look, I appreciate your suggestions, Jace, but we're wasting time. I won't let Beckham get near the interstate."

"Neither will I," he said. "I'll handle it. You stay put. Do you hear me?"

What was it with her and her silence?

"Lacey?"

"Yeah, I hear you, but if someone isn't here within the next ten minutes, Jace, I'm going after him myself."

Before he could reprimand his headstrong sister, again, she hung up on him.

Shit.

He shot to his feet and did the only thing he could do—punched the number into his phone. "Hey, Jesse…"

Saturday afternoon, Holly was at The Creamery, cleaning out the last of the cupboards and organizing them for better storage. At least, that was her story, and she was sticking to it. Her restlessness had absolutely nothing to do with keeping busy so she didn't think about a sexy-as-sin doctor and his magical hands. Or the fact she'd only spoken to him twice since those magical hands had been on her body last weekend.

Nope. That was definitely not the reason for cleaning the shop from top to bottom all week. Fall cleaning. She wanted to make sure the shop was in ship shape before she went back to Colorado, because, yeah, she was sure to be leaving soon. After all, her uncle was making remarkable progress.

"I know there's a CMP here with my name on it."

"Mine, too."

She turned to find Shayla and Caitlin smiling at her from the other side of the counter. Grinning, she straightened and rushed around to give her friends a hug. She hadn't seen either all week. The newlywed had an excuse. Honeymoon with her gorgeous husband. But did this week have to be the week Caitlin had to stay on campus to prepare for a presentation in one of her classes?

Of course it did. Left to her own devices, she worried about her job at the ski resort, having called but not gotten a return on the message, and if Jace thought about the great sex they'd had. And if he wanted more.

She did. A lot. And wanted to…a lot.

Which was bad. Very bad. And a good reason to keep busy.

"Ah, look at you, Mrs. Dalton, all sunshine and smiles," she said, pulling her friend in for a hug, secretly jealous as hell at the look of utter satisfaction oozing from the woman's lazy grin. "I don't have to ask if you had a good time. Your expression says it all."

Caitlin snorted. "I know. Are you as jealous as me?"

"Big time," she replied with a grin, releasing Shayla to hug her sister. "Okay." She drew back. "I'll get the sundaes, you head to the table in the corner where my laptop is all set up for you to check out some awesome photographs of a certain wedding I attended last week."

The redhead squealed, sending poor, unsuspecting Donny two feet in the air…along with the soft cone in his hand. The ice cream landed on the floor before his feet touched back down. He slapped a hand to his chest, and the other to the counter for support as he stared down at the splattered pumpkin spice.

"Oh, Donny. I'm so sorry," Shayla said, rushing forward. "Let me help you—"

"No! You shouldn't be bending." He thrust a hand out to keep the woman away from the spill. "I'll get it. I'm becoming an old pro. Just ask Holly. This makes the third one this week."

The sweet guy sounded as if it was something to be proud of, so she nodded with a smile. "Okay…if you're sure."

Holly stepped close. "Yes, unless you'd rather clean the floor instead of looking at photos of your wedding."

Shayla straightened. "Donny, you're on your own." Then twisted around to march toward the laptop.

They spent the next hour eating ice cream and discussing their favorite photos. When they came to the ones she'd shot of Jace, laughing at something Kade had said, her insides warmed and got all soft and mushy, like the sundae melting in her cup.

She glanced up to find Shayla and Caitlin staring at her. "What?"

"Oh. My. God." The newlywed blinked accusingly at her. "You slept with Jace."

"What?" She reeled back, happy to note the shop was empty and Donny was too far away to hear.

"You *did*." Now Caitlin was smiling. "You totally did."

Denial was on the tip of her tongue, but the damn heat flooding her face gave her away. So, she did the only thing she could at that point. Shoved more ice cream in her mouth before clicking on the next picture.

Dammit. More Jace.

Click. Click.

Dammit.

Where the hell *are the shots of the bride and groom?*

"Give it up," Shayla said with a chuckle.

Her sister nodded and leaned forward. "And tell us how it was."

She sighed and let the memory flood her. "Better than chocolate."

"I'm not surprised." The newlywed pointed at her with a spoon. "You two have some serious chemistry going on."

"Yeah, but it was only for one night. We both agreed it was for the best that way."

Shayla sighed and shook her head. "Only for the moment."

"What do you mean?"

"That is the same thing Kevin and I agree on. But one week later we fell back into bed."

Her pulse kicked up at the thought of more nights like that with Jace. Her body was totally on board and happy dancing with that, but her mind was doing the 'hell no' shuffle. "No. It'll be just the one night."

Caitlin sighed. "Yeah. I only had one night like that."

Holly's heart nose-dived for the floor. She knew her friend had gone out with Jace a few times last spring, but she never really thought the two had slept together.

"No. Not with Jace," Caitlin rushed to say, apparently reading Holly's mind. "Jace and I are just friends. Kind of like you and Tanner. Unless you've slept with Tanner."

"No. We're just friends. So then, who was your better-than-chocolate night with?"

"Keiffer Wyne," Shayla answered, then laughed when her sister's head snapped in her direction. "You already admitted to us you'd slept with him, remember?"

"Oh, yeah. That's right." Caitlin smiled, face turning a bright pink. "Must be something about weddings that make us give into…you know…*urges*," she said, before shoving the last of the ice cream in her mouth.

"Then I'm so glad no one else is getting married around here," a female said from behind.

She turned toward the voice.

Shit.

Jace's sister.

Holly recognized the dark-haired, blue-eyed beauty from the reception. *Damn.* She hoped the woman hadn't been there long enough to hear *all* of the conversation.

"Lacey! Hi," Caitlin exclaimed. "Pull up a chair."

"Yeah, we're looking at my wedding photos, eating chocolate ice cream, and discussing great sex."

Holly shot to her feet. "What can I get you?"

And please let it be to go.

"I'd love what you're having. Or had," the woman said, glancing at their empty dishes as she sat.

Damn.

"Okay. I'll be right back." She wasted no time putting space between talk of great sex and Jace's sister.

Stalling as long as possible, she made the CMP. Cleaned up. Took the trash outside to the dumpster. Washed her hands. Then finally carried the dessert back to the table and sat.

Why couldn't a family of ten walk in? Or a bus load of tourists? Or…

"Jace?" Holly shot to her feet again, refusing to look at the women as she did her best to deal with the rush of strange emotions flooding her body.

"Hi, Holly," he replied, gaze settling on her.

The last time she'd seen the sexy doctor, she'd had her naked body twisted around him like a pretzel, while she cried out his name as he thrust deep inside her. The two times she'd talked to him since then had been on the phone. In a text.

This was different. Way different.

She had the heat in her face to prove it.

His had a layer of exhaustion over the tension dulling his smile and thinning his talented mouth.

The urge to lean close and soothe the stress from his lips with her tongue was so strong, she grabbed the dirty dishes from the table to keep her body from reacting to his nearness without her permission.

"I came for my sister."

His words sank in, hitting her like a bucket of ice water.

Chapter Eleven

Lacey frowned. "I just got here."

Holly managed to nod before she turned and walked to the sink behind the counter, talking the stupid burning from her eyes.

Of course Jace isn't here for me. Why would he be? Just because they'd had great sex. Better than great sex. Amazing sex. That was no reason for him to seek her out. It wasn't like they were in a relationship.

She was such a dweeb.

With her back turned, she concentrated on stacking the dishwasher and reining in her unwanted emotions. The handsome doctor had been up front with her. Never made any promises. It was her stupid body's fault for thinking…

A warm hand touched her arm, and she jumped, twisting to find Jace had followed.

"I wasn't finished," he said, crowding her against the sink. "I was saying I came for my sister, but was hoping to see you."

"Oh." She blinked, surprised at how much better she suddenly felt.

"Yeah, *oh*," he repeated, lifting a hand to brush a strand of hair off her face. "Sorry I haven't had a chance to see you sooner."

It wasn't as if they were a couple, or even in any kind of relationship, and yet, the fact he'd thought about her enough to want to see her again sent a rush of warmth through her veins.

"This week has been extra busy," he added, the stress lines reappearing on his face. "And I have drill this weekend."

Before Holly could stop herself, she smoothed a line near his left temple with her finger. "It's okay."

Surprise and heat mixed to light his gaze. "It is now," he said, reaching up to touch the hand she held by his face.

Warmth spread through her chest, and she could feel herself grinning like a fool, despite the fact three awfully quiet women were looking on with interest from the corner of the shop. He leaned closer and opened his mouth, but whatever he'd been about to say was cut off by the ringing of the phone attached to his belt.

Releasing her, he blew out a breath and reached for his cell. "Excuse me," he said, and with an apologetic nod, he walked away to answer the call.

Instead of rejoining the girls at the table, Holly busied herself at the ice cream counter, waiting until he ended his conversation.

"Here," she said, shoving a waffle cone at him, filled with pistachio ice cream.

His favorite.

Longing entered his gaze as he stared at the treat. "Thanks, but I'm meeting with another doctor on a consult."

"Trust me," she said, lowering her voice for his ears only. "You'll have this finished before you even get to your office."

Hell, that talented tongue of his had finished her off in half the time.

Apparently reading her mind, he smiled, gaze heating to indecent as he lifted the cone to his mouth and licked.

Her insides quivered.

Dammit.

"Lacey," he said, gaze still fixed to hers. "I'll be back to get you in a half-hour."

"Okay. Take your time."

The man was good at that, too. Taking his time. Keeping her on the brink. Driving her mad before bringing her release with mind-blowing force.

"What do I owe you?"

She cleared her dried throat. "It's on the house."

"Then I guess I owe you." With one last lap of his ice cream, he turned around and left the shop with a smile on his face and a spring in his step that hadn't been there when he'd walked in.

Holly did her best to keep calm and cool on the outside, while her insides were a mass of lava overflowing to all her good parts.

If the women had noticed, they were kind enough to keep it to themselves. When she finally rejoined them, with a tall glass of ice water, she answered questions about her pictures, and ignored their knowing grins. Nope. Not going there. She kept the focus on the photos, giving her recommendations for the final album, before having to get up to wait on Connor who stopped in to order two large vanilla cones for his Kerri, while carrying a large jar of pickles.

Some of the crazy things he'd said his wife craved were similar to concoctions she'd witnessed Shayla eating the past few weeks. She was still smiling after the cowboy had gone.

"You have a great eye for photos, Holly," Lacey said, walking slowly to the counter, as if she had something on her mind. "Would you possibly be interested in photographing me on my horse? I'd be happy to pay you. He's a beauty. I don't have anything near as polished as the photos you take, and I'd really love one of me and Beckham."

"Beckham?" Her brows rose. "Like the soccer player?"

"Yep. They both have great muscle tone."

Holly laughed. "I'd love to."

"Super! Thank you so much," the woman gushed, face lighting with pure joy.

They settled on a time and price, and Lacey had just finished writing down the address when Jace walked in.

"Ready?" he asked his sister, looking even more tired and haggard than before.

Lacey nodded. "Yep." Then turned to wave good-bye to the sisters still sitting at the corner table.

Jace smiled ruefully at her, his heated gaze lingering on her lips before he followed his sister out the door.

"We'd better get going, too." Shayla yawned, rising to her feet, suddenly looking as exhausted as the doctor. "Thanks for showing me the photos. Kevin and I will be by tomorrow to officially pick them out."

"Okay," she said, coming around the counter to hug both women.

"Enjoy your weekend," Caitlin said. "Because, judging by that hungry look in Jace's eyes, the two of you *will* be *enjoying* the weekend before it's over."

Her body was completely on board, while part of her mind still held out, maintaining it was foolish to get involved with someone from Texas when she would be heading back to Colorado any day now.

That argument was getting old, and even though it was undoubtedly true, at the moment, recalling how wonderful she'd felt last Sunday, she was willing to steal a few more moments with him.

Sunday afternoon, Jace was in his office at the armory, going through periodic health assessments when Jesse strode in and dropped down into a chair. No need to ask the man how he was doing. The scowl pretty much covered it. Bad day.

"Haven't had the opportunity to thank you for throwing me under the bus the other day," his friend said, sarcasm so thick his words stuck in the air.

He sat back in his chair and raised a brow. "You're welcome?"

"Dick," Jesse muttered. "I'm talking about your sister and having to fetch her damn horse."

"Oh. That." His head tipped back, bells finally going off in his head. "Yeah, sorry. I didn't have anyone else to call. Thanks again. According to Lacey, it went okay, and you weren't *too* annoying," he said, then added, "and that's a direct quote."

"It's a miracle. I'm so relieved, for once, I actually pleased *Her Highness*." Jesse snickered.

Jace shrugged. "Why don't you just ask her out already? The two of you have been circling each other for years."

"Your sister's mean, Jace. And she's gotten worse since the accident. Big control freak."

He cocked his head and grinned. "So, you admit you're too much of a pansy-ass to handle her?"

"Fuck, yeah!" The frowning man straightened in his chair. "That's exactly what I'm saying. I value my nuts. Don't need her handing them to me every time she doesn't get her way."

Jace smiled, shaking his head, even though he was in total agreement.

"When're *you* going to grow a pair?"

"I can handle my sister just fine." Most days.

Jesse shook his head. "Not Lacey. You and Holly."

"What do you mean?"

Jesus, he hoped this wasn't about her and Tanner.

"When are you going to ask her out?" Arms folded across his chest, the soldier tilted his head and narrowed his dark gaze on him. "Or is sleeping with her enough?"

He shot forward in his chair. "I don't think that's any of your damn business."

Jesse held up his hands. "I'm not asking for a blow by blow. You know me better than that. I'm just saying she's good for you. Whenever you're around her, you smile. You should think about being around her more."

He did think about it. Every damn day. That was the problem.

"And before you try to bring up DWB, that isn't going to happen for months yet. You can't resign your commission here until the end of March. No reason you can't enjoy each other's company in the meantime. A lot can happen in five months."

He slumped back in his chair. "It's complicated."

"Then un-complicate it."

Could it really be that simple?

He pinched the bridge of his nose, but the heavy pressure in his temples remained. It was no use. He was too tired to think straight. All he wanted was to relax and not worry about work, family, or drill. All he wanted was Holly.

An hour later, Jace was still contemplating that when he pulled into his driveway and got out, stunned, thinking his thoughts had formed into reality. Holly's car was parked next to his sister's in front of the main house. Sunday evenings, his mother played bridge over at Mrs. Avery's, and sometimes his sister did, too. Apparently, not today.

Curiosity led his combat boots up the drive, but the sound of the women laughing on the side of the barn had him switching directions.

It had been a very long time since he heard Lacey laugh with her whole heart. No sarcasm or bitterness. Just joy. It sounded great, and his own lips curved into a smile. But when he rounded the corner, all the euphoria evaporated as wave of white, hot anger shook through him.

"Lacey! What the hell is wrong with you? Get off the damn horse!" His voice boomed in the air, echoing off the barn, scaring the women who jumped…and startled the horse.

Beckham lurched forward, sending his sister backward.

Chapter Twelve

Jace lunged toward his sister, but was too far away and too late. His heart shot to his throat, while he watched her fall, as if in slow motion, to the hard dirt ground.

"*Lacey,*" Holly cried, racing forward to kneel beside her. "Are you all right?"

"Don't move," he ordered, bending over his sister, pressing his stubborn sibling back as she made to sit up.

She brushed his hands away. "I'm fine. And I have to get Beckham."

"Let your brother check you out," Holly said, her voice stern. "I'll get your horse. You stay put." She didn't move away until Lacey reluctantly nodded.

He was too worried to be surprised at how easily his sister complied. His chest was so tight he could barely breathe, but he tuned everything out and began his examination.

"I'm okay. Honest," his patient insisted. "My hip is a little sore. Not my back."

A few minutes later, he concurred, but pulled the phone from his belt and called an ambulance anyway.

"Really, Jace?" Lacey glared at him, still lying flat on her back. "I don't need a damn ambulance, and I do *not* want to see the inside of another hospital room."

"Too damn bad." He glared right back, his voice low and rough as his anger returned. "You should've thought of that before getting on that damn horse."

"Oh, for goodness sakes, Jace. I was fine until you got here."

"Fine? You were on the damn horse."

"Yeah, getting my picture taken. That's all. I was not riding him."

He stared at her, his mind replaying the scene in his head. Lacey had been on the horse, smiling at Holly…and the camera in the woman's hands.

Well…hell.

He shook his head. "Doesn't matter. Sitting on him is just as dangerous. What the hell were the two of you thinking?"

"Hey, wait a minute. Holly had nothing to do with this. I asked her to come here and take the pictures. She doesn't know about my back."

He considered that moment, then nodded. "But you know how dangerous it is, Lacey. Why do you insist on pushing yourself?" Then his heart lurched as a thought occurred. "Who saddled him?"

"No one. I'm not stupid," she said. "He was bareback…and we really need to go get him."

"No worries. I got him," Holly said, rounding the corner, fingers entwined in the horse's dark mane.

His mouth dropped open as stupor momentarily took over, followed by a bit of admiration. "How the hell…"

No one but Lacey, Jesse, and Kade were able to get near the horse, let alone get the spirited animal to cooperate, especially without a bridle.

She ran her hand up and down the contour of muscles on Beckham's side. "He's just a big softie for some sweet-talking, aren't you boy?"

The horse answered with a snort, and his sister relaxed as Holly led the huge animal into the barn. Despite the circumstances, his body remembered the feel of the woman's soft, sure touch when she'd stroked him with those gifted hands.

"Your girlfriend has a way with stubborn males." Lacey laughed, then stiffened at the sound of the approaching ambulance.

It was on the tip of his tongue to tell her Holly wasn't his girlfriend, but then the paramedics rushed over, and he was too busy filling them in. Two minutes later, still wearing his ACUs and a week's worth of exhaustion, he rushed across the driveway so he could follow the ambulance in his truck.

If he survived what was left of the weekend, it would be a miracle.

Ten-thirty that night, Holly had given up trying to find something on television that would hold her attention. It was no use. She was worried about Lacey, especially after she came out of the barn to see the ambulance heading down the drive and the taillights of Jace's truck as he followed.

She'd rushed to the hospital, but since she wasn't family, the emergency room staff wouldn't tell her anything. After hanging around for an hour without even a glimpse of Jace, she left. The ride back to her cottage was a bit of a blur, and somehow she ended up at The Creamery, where Donny, of all people, filled her in about Lacey's riding accident earlier that year.

If anything happened to the woman to set her back…or worse, Holly would never forgive herself. No wonder Jace was so furious. She hadn't understood why he was so upset when it was obvious his sister was okay.

Now…God…now, she understood. And if…

A knock on the door stopped her mid-thought, and she rushed to answer.

Her heart lurched at the sight of Jace, still dressed in his army camouflage uniform, face drawn and tight. But, a little light sparked in his eyes when he saw her.

"Hi," he said. "Sorry to stop in so late, but I saw your light on and thought maybe you'd be up for some company.

"Of course." She grabbed his arm and tugged him inside, leading him straight to the couch where she pulled him to sit down. "How's Lacey? I swear, Jace. I had no idea about her back. If I'd have known…" Her voice trailed off as all the emotions of the day hit her at once.

She swiped at the tears that suddenly appeared, but he cupped her face with both hands and used his thumbs to wipe them away.

"It's all right. She's fine," he said softly. "I took her home, then drove back here. She wanted me to call you, but I didn't want to talk on the phone. I wanted to see you."

A smile tugged her lips as she reached up to smooth her fingers over the left side of his temple. "I'm glad. I wanted to see you, too. Have you eaten anything?"

"Yeah. I had something that tasted like cardboard at the hospital while we waited for all the scans."

She chuckled. "Sounds yummy. Want me to make you something? I promise it'll taste better than cardboard."

Heat suddenly entered his gaze, and his hands left her face to trail down the sides of her body. "I'm only hungry for one thing."

"Oh?"

"Yeah," he replied, pushing her down into the cushions. "You."

Her heart skipped a beat, then rocked against her ribs when he lowered his mouth to hers. No need to ask if he was too tired. He seemed to have gotten a second wind, because he had a hand under her shirt, gliding up her side. Her body quivered in anticipation, waiting for more.

He gave her more. Much more. His thumb brushed her nipple through the lace, then suddenly his hand was underneath her, unhooking her bra.

Jace drew back, pushed her loose clothing up and glanced at her bare chest, gaze darkening to a delicious cobalt blue. "So perfect," he said, before capturing her nipple in his mouth.

She arched up, clutching his head, crying out when his hand covered the other breast, flicking the taut peak back and forth.

This is where Jace had wanted to be all damn week. In Holly's arms. This was total and utter perfection. He kissed his way to her other nipple, his body tight with need, already nearing his breaking point as she writhed and moaned under him.

"Jace."

She clawed at the buttons on his jacket, so he released her and lifted up enough to finish, yanking it off, followed by his T-shirt, before going back down on her delicious body. At the contact of skin on skin, she gasped and latched her mouth on his shoulder. Her sexy, breathy sounds zinged right through him, and when her fingers trailed down his abs and snuck between them to unbutton the top of his pants he nearly lost it.

"You're killing me," he murmured against her skin as he trailed kisses over her collarbone and throat, while he grabbed her hands to hold them over her head.

"Well, you make me—"

She sucked in a breath when he zeroed in on the peaks beckoning for attention. Licking her nipples, he reached down to unhook her jeans, muttering a curse when her hands were suddenly back between their bodies, brushing his erection as she unzipped his pants. He jerked, and the movement sent them tumbling the short space onto the floor.

Twisting so he'd take the brunt and land on his back, he circled his arms around her and held her to his chest. Air whooshed from his lungs on contact.

"Are you okay?" she asked, pushing off him to stare down, green gaze full of heat and concern.

He shook his head. "No. We have on too many clothes."

She laughed, smacking his arm before straddling him. "Is this better?" she asked, shrugging out of her opened shirt, followed by her bra.

Ah hell... "Yeah, so much better."

Her breasts gave a delicious bounce, and he immediately reached up to cup them.

"Mmm…" She closed her eyes as she leaned forward a little, filling his hands with more of her softness.

But just as he was about to flip their positions, she suddenly moved back to kneel between his legs and yanked his pants and boxers to the middle of his thighs. His erection sprang free, and heaven help him, her eyes dilated and gaze grew deliciously wicked before her fingers curled around him, and she took him in her mouth.

"Fuck." His head thunked the floor and eyes rolled back.

She felt good. *So damn good*. But if she didn't stop soon.

Jace reached for her, grabbing her shoulders. "Holly. Stop." He groaned as she upped her pace. "But *I* owe *you.*"

She pushed him back down with her hand. "No," she murmured against his tip. "You relax. Let me take care of you."

And before he could respond, her lips descended around him again.

Her mouth was warm and moist, and just watching her go down on him melted his backbone. He let out a husky groan, vowing to make it up to her later. Right now, he did as he was told. Closing his eyes, he relaxed against the floor, and let the incredible woman take care of him.

Within minutes, she shredded his control. His hands were in her hair, holding her head, need, desperate and hot, taking over. "Ah…yeah…Holly," was all he managed as a warning as he felt everything tighten.

She hummed in response, and that was his undoing.

Gripping the back of her head, he thrust up into her and blew apart, so hard and so fast he saw spots…and his damn eyes were closed. When she finally released him, he was blissfully exhausted, and totally boneless. She crawled up his body, and he mustered enough strength to pull her into his arms and smile when she settled against his chest.

"I hope that helped relieve some of your stress," she murmured, her breath warm on his skin.

His smile broadened. "And then some," he replied, and he kissed the top of her head.

And as soon as he grabbed just a little bit of shut eye, he'd return the favor. In spades.

The following Sunday, Holly found herself at the Dalton ranch carving pumpkins and smiling at the enthusiasm lighting Amelia's face as the little girl chirped about the princess costume her daddy bought her for Halloween.

"And I'm going to be the bestest superhero ever," the girl's cousin, Cody, proudly announced.

His mother, Jen, gave him a pat on his back. "Of that I have no doubt," she said and received a thumbs up.

The children's joy and excitement brought back fond memories for Holly. Of her childhood and how this was a favorite time of the year for her and her brother. They might not have had a lot of money, but her mother had always made the costume of their choice, and took them trick-or-treating the second their neighbor's porch lights turned on.

Nowadays, parents took their children out during the day to merchants and parties, instead.

"I hope you stop by the shop on Halloween," she told them. "Because I have treat bags."

This won her an enthusiastic cheer before Jen ushered the kids into the kitchen to clean up before supper.

"Sometimes I get tired just listening to those two," Shayla said, stifling a yawn. "I can't imagine adding another to the mix."

She eyed her friend, looking for signs of stress or tension, but the pregnant woman smiled sweetly as she rubbed her starting to show baby bump of a tummy. "I'm sure it'll be great."

"Speaking of great," her friend said, glancing around as if to make sure they were alone before she continued. "Tell me, how long did it take?"

She frowned, not following. "What do you mean?"

"For you and Jace to fall into bed again."

Oh, that. Apparently, something in her expression must've given her away, because Shayla smiled and wore an I-told-you-so grin.

"One week, wasn't it?" her friend asked as they carried the Jack-o-lanterns outside to the porch.

No sense in denying it. "Yeah." And they had an unexpected rendezvous when she met him for lunch at his office on Wednesday.

"Don't beat yourself up about it." Shayla set the small pumpkin on the railing. "Sometimes the best of intentions are often the best foundations."

She was still digesting the poetic words when her body experienced the best of sensations. Jace was near. She knew without turning around. Heat skittered down her spine and branched out in a warm shiver in all directions.

He and a few guardsmen had spent the day helping Kade finish the shelter barn for tomorrow, when the Humane Society relocated two more neglected horses to Shadow Rock.

"Wow, these look great," he said, ambling up the porch. "You've been busy."

She laughed, lifting her face to his when he bent down to give her a kiss. "The kids did these. We're just the deliverers."

"Ah," Kevin said, coming up the steps. "Well, you two have great delivery." He kissed Shayla's cheek and gently touched her belly. "And you will be greatly delivered next spring."

"You're a goof." His wife knocked him playfully on the arm.

"That may be, but I am right."

"Yes, you are."

"Could you put that in writing, darlin'? Sometimes it's hard to convince bossman of that. Although, Cole has gotten better at listening."

"He has to in order to keep up with Jordan," Jace said before turning to her. "You ready to head out?"

Judging by the gleam in his eyes, he was ready to head in…to her. And just like that, she was damp.

She nodded, and after a round of good-byes and thanks for the help handshakes and hugs, she climbed into Jace's truck with anticipation upping her pulse. By the time they pulled into her driveway, her whole body was a mass of tingling nerves.

It was weird how they only seemed to spend Sunday nights together, but given their uncertain future, she felt one night a week was probably best. Then Shayla's words about best of intentions and best of foundations flittered through her mind. But thoughts of foundations were a bit scary and too permanent for whatever it was they were doing.

Not once had Jace said anything remotely resembling the word relationship. Which was fine with her. And the fact they spent time at her little cottage and not once at his place told her she wasn't likely to hear the 'R' word from him anytime soon. Which was okay. Her time in Harland County was coming to an end. With her uncle's recovery back on track, it was fairly safe to assume he'd be given the green light to go back to work after his next appointment.

Again, the lack of commitment was fine with her. Fun, and blowing off steam. That was their main focus.

"So…" He turned to her as soon as they entered her cottage and shut the door. "Can I interest you in taking a shower? I promise to wash your back if you wash mine."

She laughed, going easily into his arms when he pulled her near. “Don’t you mean scratch?”

“That, too,” he said, nuzzling her neck.

She was doing her best not to cross her eyes as her body melted against him.

“Mmm…you smell like pumpkin and spice.”

“If you say *and everything nice* I may have to hurt you.”

“Oh.” He chuckled. “So, you want to be bad…”

Holly drew back and stared up into his teasing gaze. “You know you like when I’m bad.”

And to prove it, she trailed a finger down his chest, over his flat abs, and traced the bulge in his jeans, lingering near the tip.

He groaned and pulled her close, bringing his mouth down on hers, kissing her with a hunger and intensity she was beginning to crave more than air. Who was she kidding? There was no *beginning to* about it.

His hot kisses were the first thing she thought about in the mornings, and the last thing she thought about before bed. So, when he bent down and lifted her up in his arms before carrying her to the bathroom, all while his mouth continued to pull her apart at the seams, she considered *this* to be his best intention of the day.

Chapter Thirteen

The next morning, Jace awoke to the best smell in the world.

Bacon.

Opening his eyes, he witnessed to the best sight in the world.

Holly wearing nothing but his unbuttoned shirt, carrying a tray of food.

"Morning," she said with a smile. "Thought you could use some sustenance after our four a.m. go round."

He sat up against the pillows, oddly touched. "Thanks, but you didn't have to do this, Holly."

"I know," she said, leaning in to kiss him on the lips. "I wanted to. You deserve breakfast in bed, once in a while."

He caught her hand when she made to leave, and brought it to his lips. "I already had breakfast in bed at four a.m., remember?"

Heat skittered through her gaze and turned her grin wicked. She tugged free, but leaned close, giving him a glimpse of paradise under his parted shirt. "If I say no, will you refresh my memory after we recharge with breakfast? Or do you have to leave for the office?"

He shot his gaze to the clock on her bedside table, surprised he hadn't even thought about work. And it was a Monday, his busiest morning of the week. Luck was on his side. He wasn't scheduled for another two hours.

"I have some time yet," he said, scooting over so she could join him.

Together, they enjoyed the scrambled eggs and bacon she'd cooked.

Starting the day off with a bang appealed to him. Big time. *Damn*, he hadn't had sex before work at the beginning of the week in well…never. Just like he'd never had a woman cook him breakfast and bring it to him in bed. This woman was more than happy to do both. And without being asked.

"Thanks for breakfast," he said again, liking the way her gaze softened when she stared into his eyes.

"You're always helping others. I wanted to pamper you for a change."

Something actually fluttered in his chest. "Thanks," he said, placing the tray of empty plates on the side table before turning back to face her. "I appreciate it. But, what I want is you."

Her intake of breath cooled the air between. They stared at each other a beat, then they were kissing, gentle at first, then not so gentle. Her hands were suddenly as hungry and desperate as her kiss, pulling him on top of her, making him instantly hard and throbbing.

He spread the shirt open, and had just sucked one beautiful, tight nipple into his mouth when a phone rang.

It took them both a second to realize it was her phone.

"Sorry," she muttered, reaching for the cell on the table by the other side of her bed.

"Maybe they'll call back." He trailed kisses down her belly, which was now eye level.

Her warm body stiffened under his lips. He glanced up to see apprehension replace the desire in her eyes.

"It's work. Colorado work," she informed before rolling off the bed to answer the call.

She walked into the living room, but since the place was small, he could still hear her muffled voice. Even though he wanted to give her privacy, her dejected tone had him off the bed, slipping into his discarded jeans and heading into the other room.

"Yeah. No. I understand." She was nodding as if the person on the other end of the phone could actually see her. "Thanks. I appreciate the call. I will. Bye."

She hung up, and stood with her back to him, her shoulders hunched, long sigh leaving her body. He walked around her dejected form to peer into her face.

"Bad news?"

She blinked at him and let out another sigh. "That was a heads up for the termination letter I will be receiving in the mail this week."

Ah, hell.

He opened his arms, and after a few beats of hesitation, stepped close and wrapped her arms around his back. He wasn't too great at this stuff, but knew she needed something. Holding her close, he ran his hands up and down her back, offering some lame-ass words of comfort that more than likely meant jack-shit.

The poor, giving woman just lost the job she'd busted her ass to secure, and all because she had a soft heart, and strong sense of family.

She didn't cry, though, or sniff, just stood there quietly holding him and letting him hold her. Thank God. He wasn't any good at handling tears, either. As a physician, yes. As a friend, lover, comforting another, no.

"Oh well," she said, releasing him and moving out of his arms to busy herself with the dirty frying pan at the sink in the quaint, open kitchen. "I knew it was only a matter of time. They'd been way more than fair. I mean, my three month leave-of-absence is now going on five. I'd fire my ass, too."

Her words were clear and delivered with humor, but he could hear the underlying disappointment and worry in every one.

Jace stepped into the kitchen and helped himself to a coffee from her machine. And since she'd obviously given this a lot of thought, he felt it was safe to ask. "What will you do now?"

"I've asked myself that question for a few weeks, because I assumed this was going to happen. But, I've yet to come up with an answer. I needed that job, Jace. Dammit. I needed that pay. I'm kind of supporting two households. I'm not sure how I'll help my mom or brother now."

He set his mug down and stepped close to brush the hair back from her temple. "If anyone can come up with a solution, you can. And you know I'm always around if you need to bounce ideas."

She smiled. "Thanks. I appreciate it. But, you have enough on your plate. And you're right. I'll figure something out."

The urge to pull her back into his arms was strong, but something in the closed off look in her eyes held him back. There was a barrier there now. A distance that hadn't existed a half-hour ago.

She slipped out of his shirt and handed it back to him. "You should go. I don't want to make you late for work."

Sounded like a heave ho. Although he hated to leave her after she suffered such a blow, and looked so damn hot walking buck naked back to her room, he couldn't stay. He had patients counting on him. "Yeah. I know," he said, slipping into his shirt and following her, his groin as stiff as her shoulders as he watched her pull on sweats and a T-shirt. She was wearing *loner mode* like an invisible cloak. She didn't need to take on the world alone. "I just hate to leave you like this."

Her chin lifted. "I'll be fine. I always am. Now, go. Time to be the doctor everyone counts on."

He smiled and began to button his shirt. "Yes, ma'am."

She smiled back, and it almost reached her eyes. "Good. Go on now, off with you."

"How about I stop by after work and take you out to dinner?"

"Hey, you don't have to suddenly start treating me different. I mean it. I'll be fine. No need to vary from your routine."

Ouch.

But, she was right. Not once had he taken her out. Only took her body, here in her cottage, and once at his office.

Damn. It didn't feel good knowing he was such a cad. He needed to fix things.

"Maybe I want to break the routine." He had no idea where those words came from, but stood by them, because…hell…they were true. She deserved more than just an occasional romp. He was such a jackass.

She blew out a breath and walked around him. "I'm not sure that's such a good idea, Jace. We started this thing to be fun. Adding dinner out and stuff changes things."

"So, you're saying I can't care about you?" He followed her into the living room.

"No." She turned around to face him. "I'm saying I don't need pity or pity dates. An hour ago, you never once mentioned dinner tonight."

True, mostly because the sight of her naked body peeking out from under his shirt had muddled his brain cells.

And because he was an ass. A clueless one.

"It's okay. It's been fun," she said. "But, this is a good time to let it end. We're too different. It wasn't going to go anywhere anyway. You're driven, precise, about to embark on a goal you've had set in place for decades now. You have your life all planned. And that's great. Mine's not. Everything is up in the air. I'm swimming in mud with my hands tied behind my back."

She stared at him, and he got the impression she expected him to nod in agreement.

Not happening.

"Look, Holly, I think you're a little misguided about my life. You've met my sister. Seen the ranch. My practice. There's no *order* about it. There are days I feel I'm in that mud pool right beside you." Though he smiled, her expression remained solemn. That's when it hit him. He folded his arms across his chest and held her gaze. "Who was the guy who screwed you over, left you out of his plans? Was he a doctor?"

Her chin lifted slightly. "Plastic Surgeon. I thought he was different, you know? Not like my dad with his sweet charm and fake promises. And Craig *was* different, at least, at first. But when my job got important, it was suddenly only okay for him to work long hours, not me."

"He leave you?"

"No. Wanted me to quit. And when I didn't, he cheated on me with my best friend, claiming it was my fault for neglecting him."

"What a dick."

A smile twitched her lips. "That's what I called him, right before I walked out."

"Good for you. You deserve better."

"Thanks. I know," she said, slowly nodding. "I deserve to be treated like more than a warm body in bed."

Ah, hell. He felt the skewer lance straight through him.

"Holly…" He stepped closer, but she backed away, holding up her hands.

"It's okay, Jace. That's exactly how we started this thing. My eyes were completely open. I was a warm body for you to enjoy, and you were a warm one for me to enjoy right back. And we did. Our chemistry was truly great."

Past tense, he noted, with an invisible blow to the gut.

"But I don't need you feeling responsible for me because we slept together."

"You think I feel responsible for you because you came crying my name?"

A flush entered her cheeks, but her gaze remained neutral. "Yes. You can't help it. You're a healer and a helper, Jace. It's one of the things I like most about you."

Apparently, not enough to cut me some damn slack.

"Look, Holly, I know I screwed up."

"Hey." She frowned and stepped closer. "No, you did absolutely nothing wrong. We agreed on no relationship and great sex. That's exactly what you gave me, and I'm good with that. It has been great. But I know if we tried to continue on that path, one of us is going to get hurt, and I'm not about to let that happen. Too many people depend on us." She pivoted around on her bare feet and headed toward her room. "The last thing either of us needs is to be less than par. Let's just enjoy the memories."

He winced. "I appreciate what you're saying, but *not* what you're not saying."

She turned around in the doorway and frowned at him. "What do you mean?"

"You're lumping me with Craig and your dad. I'm not them, Holly. And sure as hell don't deserve to be judged by their downfalls."

Her green gaze stared unblinkingly at him. "I'm not judging you, Jace," she said quietly. "I'm cutting you loose."

And apparently, the conversation was over, because she entered her bedroom and slowly closed the door.

He stood there, staring at the door as if it had the answer to what the hell just happened?

Since it didn't, and he had no clue, he pulled on his socks and boots and let himself out, an uninvited pain gripping his chest.

By the time the second week in November rolled around, Holly had exhausted all avenues of finding a job back home. All the resorts were currently not hiring any marketing team members. She'd even inquired about regular office work. No one had an opening.

"Any luck, hun?" Uncle Arthur asked, sitting behind his desk in the office at The Creamery.

Today was his third day back, and she tried not to dwell on the fact that if he'd only gotten clearance two weeks sooner, they wouldn't be having this conversation. She'd learned long ago life was strange and things happen for a reason.

She just wished she knew what the reason was for her life to be in limbo.

"No," she replied, keeping her tone light.

"Well, my offer still stands," he reminded. "You've increased sales here by more than thirty percent."

Smiling, she sat in the chair opposite his desk, happy to discuss the small changes she'd made. "It was just a few minor adjustments."

Cutting spending, curbing wasteful uses of materials like napkins. No need to let them out on the tables. Handing each customer a napkin with their purchase hadn't saved a ton, but it did cut down, not only on supplies, but garbage removal, too.

The only place she didn't cut was uncoordinated employees. With the money spent cleaning up after Donny, or replacing equipment the poor guy accidentally broke, Holly could've hired two part time people.

But she didn't. And wouldn't. Replacing him was not an option, and he was getting better. He could actually make a milkshake without getting any ice cream on his shirt.

Now that was progress.

Her uncle leaned forward and tapped his desk. "Whatever you've been doing is great. Keep it up. I'm glad you're able to still stick around and help me out. I've only been back a few days, and even though I hate to admit it, I'm tired. I hadn't expected it to take so much out of me."

"Are you okay? Want me to take you home?" She straightened in her chair, searching his face for signs up distress. He had good color and his mouth wasn't as pinched as it had been when he'd first had the operation.

"I'm fine. Just a little tired, and not too stubborn to admit coming back to work full time is definitely more than these old bones can handle." He grinned, looking completely at ease for someone who had trouble giving up control when she'd first arrived back in March. "I'm thinking about semi-retiring and would really love for you to take over."

Holly sat in stunned silence. Her uncle just spouted two things she'd never thought she'd hear. Retirement and handing her the reins.

He chuckled. "I've rendered you speechless."

"Pretty much." She blinked, waiting for the punch line. None came. "You're seriously going to retire?"

"*Semi*-retire," he corrected, then nodded. "And, yes. I think it's more than time. Especially if someone like you takes over. I know you'll uphold my traditions, and you'll treat my lifelong customers to a quality product and service."

Donny's face flashed through her mind. She shook it off. The college student was eager to learn, and that was a Crowley standard.

"I realize your heart is in Colorado, but I'm hoping you'll give Texas a chance," he said.

Now, a dark-haired, blue-eyed doctor's face flashed through her mind. She wasn't sure if it was caused by the word Texas or heart. Or both. She had the feeling she would always think of the handsome, caring man whenever she heard either. Because he was the epitome of both.

"I actually do like it here," she admitted, shifting in her seat, a little uncomfortable with the truth in that statement, and the fact it had a lot to do with her friends in Harland County.

Including Jace.

Since the day she'd gotten fired, they hadn't had sex, but they'd hung out at gatherings or restaurants with a bunch of their friends. They even worked together as volunteers at the new animal shelter recently opened at Shadow Rock. He was patient and gentle, and she marveled at his ability to heal. She'd witnessed it multiple times, in both humans and animals.

It was a good thing they weren't still having sex, because she could definitely see herself falling for the man.

How stupid would that be?

"Holly?"

She blinked, suddenly aware her uncle had asked her a question. "I'm sorry, what did you say?

"I asked if you were going to come back to Texas after taking your mother home over the Thanksgiving holiday."

"Good question." She laughed, but it sounded forced even to her own ears. Lifting a hand, she scratched her temple and sighed. "Depends. I'm going to visit each resort and hand them my resume in person."

He nodded. "Smart. Always best to apply in person, even if there are no job listings in the paper."

"Exactly."

"Well, just remember, if that doesn't work out, I could use you here."

"Thanks," she said, wishing she could give him a definite answer. But, keeping a roof over her brother's head, and helping her mom keep her home in Denver meant Holly needed to find a higher-paying job.

Their well-being was her number one priority.

"Your mom tells me you've been doing some photography for the locals," he said, sitting back in his chair.

She nodded. So far, she'd finished three side jobs she'd gotten from people who had seen Shayla and Kevin's wedding album. "Yeah, last weekend I shot photos for a brochure for the new shelter."

"I heard Kade finally got it going. He's a good man."

She nodded again. "Yes, he is." The handsome cowboy had insisted on paying her for her time and expertise. She'd refused. Of course. She wanted to do it for the animals. But he wouldn't take no for an answer. So, as soon as the honorable man had handed her a check, she wrote out a donation to the shelter for the same amount. The animals needed it more than her at the moment. She'd figure a way to keep a roof over her head, and felt good knowing she helped keep a roof over theirs.

There was a reason she'd graduated top of her class in college. The ability to adapt had always been her strong suit. That and tenacity. Growing up with a hardworking mother who was stretched too thin, and a father who lived clear across the country and couldn't even remember a birthday, she'd needed an abundance of both.

She was still contemplating these later that night as she wiped down the soft ice cream machine, scrubbing the sticky layers of vanilla and chocolate from the surface to reveal the worn, yet strong, stainless steel underneath. She could relate. Her life was coming to a crossroads. And her uncle's semi-retirement and offer to have her run his business held infinite appeal. She could remove the layers of duty and responsibility, and stay and be happy…or find a job in her field back in Colorado and continue to support her family.

As much as she'd love to choose the first, she knew she'd always choose the latter.

"Hey, Holly," Kevin greeted, ducking as he walked into the shop with a giggling Amelia on his shoulders.

She wiped her hands on a nearby towel and smiled at the little girl and her daddy. "Well, hello there. What kind of goodies can I get for you tonight?"

Amelia thrust a tiny finger down at the case. "*Choclit.*"

"You got it, darlin'," the sweet child's daddy replied, then set the little girl down. "I've got a bunch of hungry friends and relatives outside. What do you say you hand me two vats of ice cream, while you grab, spoons and bowls, and join us?"

Before she could reply, he came around the other side of the counter and grabbed the ice cream from the case. "One vanilla and one chocolate ought to do it."

"Yay," his daughter cheered, then pointed to the paper dishes. "Bowls."

Figuring it was close enough to closing, and she could join the Dalton's for a treat, Holly handed the *mini* Shayla a small stack of cups before she grabbed another stack and a handful of spoons, unsure of how many were needed, before following the two out the door.

"Surprise!"

She stopped dead.

Half of Harland County occupied the five outdoor tables. Daltons and McCalls, Tanner and Jesse, Caitlin and even Donny. Plus Lacey…and Jace.

"You didn't think we were going to let you leave Texas without wishing you well, did you?" Shayla asked, walking over to give her a hug after Kerri took the cups and spoons from her hands and began to scoop out ice cream.

With a hot throat and burning eyes, she spent the next five minutes hugging everyone. Her true friends. And there were a lot of them. Leaving Texas was going to be damn hard.

For some reason, the quick hug she received from the quiet doctor spoke the loudest. Hurt the most, but she swallowed past the lump and tight chest, and kept her lips curved in a smile.

"Thanks for coming."

He drew back, gaze guarded but friendly. "Of course. I hope you find what you want."

Why did she feel as if she already had?

That was a crazy thought. And she couldn't afford to think them. Not one bit. Denver was home. Her family needed her. It was time to look for a job back in Colorado. It was time to forget about the warm, hard strength of the doctor still waiting for her to respond.

She widened her smile. "Ditto."

For some reason, her hot throat wouldn't allow her to say more, but it didn't matter since her mind couldn't form a longer response, or send a message to her hands to release the quiet man.

Apparently, he suffered the same brain fog, because his fingers were still wrapped around her upper arms.

Which explained the tingling.

"Well, Holly, I bet you'll be glad to see the last of me," Donny said, ambling closer, breaking the spell.

Jace released her, nodded to the young man, then joined his sister at one of the tables. Her heart squeezed so tight at the sight of his retreating form, but it didn't matter. The two of them had no future, so there was no sense in entertaining a present.

The moment Jace's boots hit the floor boards on his mother's porch, he was hit with the unmistakable, delicious aroma of her turkey. This would be his last Thanksgiving at home for a few years, so, he intended to make the most of it. Stepping inside the house out of the cool November wind, he shook off the chill and inhaled a stronger lungful. The smells of turkey, pumpkin pie, and spices filled him with an unexpected nostalgia.

He opened his eyes and could clearly picture his father sitting in the recliner, cheering for the underdog playing football on television, while his mother and sister put the finishing touches on a dinner they'd talk about for days.

Good times.

"There you are." His mother stopped whatever she'd been doing at the counter to walk over and kiss his cheek. "I figured the smells would tempt you up here sooner or later."

"You know it. What can I do to help?"

"Nothing. You do too much the way it is. You deserve to relax and be pampered for a change."

His mother's words triggered memories of a dark-haired, green-eyed woman who'd told him nearly the same thing over a month ago. Even though they'd said their good-byes, he had to admit, he missed Holly.

Not just sexually, either. Sure, there was that, but he hadn't realized she'd come to mean more to him than the warm body she spoke of the morning they'd ended their…fun. He'd missed her wit and intelligence, warm smile, the kind that lit her eyes a brilliant shade of green, her caring nature and the way she laughed at herself whenever she made a mistake.

"Hey, Jace," Lacey said, breezing in from the other room. "You hear from Holly?"

He reeled back, more than a little surprised by the question. "No. We're not a couple. We're just friends," he clarified as he took a seat at the table. "Besides, I'm pretty sure she's busy looking for a job in Colorado." Something inside his chest tightened at the thought.

"That's right." Lacey nodded, taking the bowl of mashed potatoes from their mom and setting it on the table. "She did say she was going to apply to some of the resorts up there, now that Mr. Crowley's doing better."

His mother smiled over her shoulder. "Oh, good for Arthur. I'm glad he's doing better. Life is tough when you're restricted."

"Tell me about it." His sister snorted as she set a bowl of sweet potatoes next to the green bean casserole.

His stomach growled in anticipation of sampling a heaping portion of everything.

"Do you think Holly will stay in Colorado?" his mother asked.

He shrugged. "I don't know."

But he did know he didn't like the thought of not seeing the woman again. Something inside his chest shifted, and he had a hard time breathing.

"She told me it would depend on if she found a job up there," Lacey informed. "Would it make me a terrible person if I said I hope she doesn't?"

I'd be terrible right next to you, he thought, trying to keep from losing his appetite.

"I like her, Jace," she told him simply.

"Me, too," his mother said. "But is there a reason for this conversation?"

He shook his head at the same time Lacey nodded.

"Yeah. Jace needs a swift kick in the…"

"Lacey Jane!" His mother frowned down at his sister who had the good sense to look remorseful.

"Sometimes, those are the only words that get through to your stubborn son, Mama."

"I'm right here," he said, waving his hand, tired of being talked about in the third person. "You can talk directly to me."

Lacey turned her unswerving gaze on him. "Okay, Jace. I was just going to say *fix* whatever happened between you and Holly."

"Nothing happened because there was nothing between us." Even as the words left his mouth, he knew they were full of shit. At least, on his part. He did feel something for Holly. It hadn't been his intention, but it had happened anyway.

He cared about her.

He missed her.

He hoped like hell he got a chance to see her again.

"Bullsh…" Lacey cleared her throat. "Phewy. The two of you could barely take your eyes off each other."

"True." His mother nodded. "I saw how you two stared at each other at the Dalton wedding. Life is too short to ignore an attraction like that, Jace. Some people aren't even lucky enough to have the opportunity. You shouldn't blow yours."

His sister smiled. "Exactly. So, at least think about it if she comes back here, ya goof. She's good for you. You're a lot nicer when she's around."

"So, *that's* what this is about. You." A smile tugged his lips.

"Of course," she responded to his teasing with a grin. "Life is so much easier to deal with when you're not grumpy around here."

"Me?" He chuckled. "Same goes for you, sis. Life is smoother when you're not grumpy."

"You're both right," his mother cut in. "Life is always better when my kids are happy. And have full bellies. So, what do you say? Don't you think it's time for Jace to carve this turkey?"

With a desire to make this Thanksgiving a fun, memorable one, he filed away thoughts of Holly and focused on the other two important women in his life. And as the three of them talked about what they were most thankful for, Jace vowed that, if Holly did return to Harland County, he would try to *fix* things between them.

Chapter Fourteen

It was a little strange to be in Denver with her mother and brother, sitting at her mother's kitchen table, enjoying a slice of apple pie after an amazing Thanksgiving dinner. The laughter, sights, sounds, and smells surrounded her in an invisible, warm hug.

And she was cold.

She shivered, blaming it on the six inches of new snow that had fallen that day. She was home. Close to ski slopes, and lodges, and a snow pack her inner ski demon normally salivated over.

Not this time.

"It's so great to have my children with me for probably our last Thanksgiving together for a while," her mother said, reaching out to squeeze her and her brother's hands. "Next year, I'll be in Texas, Zach will probably be in a country that doesn't even celebrate the holiday, and you'll be here alone, Holly. Unless you move down to Texas, too."

She blinked. "Wait…what?"

Since when was her mother moving to Texas?

Her brother chuckled. "Mom, you probably should've started by telling Holly you were moving in with Uncle Arthur when your lease runs out next month. And I'll be moving in with my friend Joe before I leave for Japan in December. He has an apartment near the university."

Holly blinked at her brother. "Wait…what?"

"Need me to run through it again, sis?"

"I need a moment for this to sink in," she said, transferring her gaze to her smiling mother. "You're moving in with Uncle Arthur?"

"Yep. We've discussed it a lot the past few months. Neither of us is getting younger, and it was really nice to reconnect."

Holly could understand that. Just the two days she'd been back in Denver, she'd enjoyed being around her brother, surprised at how much she'd missed his upbeat attitude and ready grin.

"Mom," she reached out to touch her arm as a thought occurred. "You're not doing this because of me, are you? I mean, moving is big enough, but uprooting to another state, leaving your friends behind. Are you sure?"

"I'm positive. And I'm doing it for both of us. I don't want you to worry about me anymore. It's time your brother and I made our own way. You need to live your own life.

"We *each* need to do that," Zach said.

"So, no more helping me pay my lease," her mother told her. "Your uncle owns his house free and clear, so I won't even have to pay anything to stay there. He's insisting I just move in and enjoy myself for a change."

"And no more having to pay an exorbitant amount of rent so I can be close to college, Hol. We don't need that place. Besides, I'll be graduating in May."

"But where will you live afterward? Will Joe let you stay?"

He smiled broadly, kind of staring at her like she was a little daft. "Yeah, but hopefully, I'll be living somewhere in Japan."

Oh. Yeah. Right.

She blew out a breath, finding her chest strangely not so tight. In fact, her shoulders felt quite a bit lighter, too.

"So, maybe you should think about moving, too. At least, out of that apartment. I know you can find somewhere cheaper in Denver. Or Aspen. Or Harland County. Wherever you choose to live."

Harland County...

Once she'd given it a chance, she'd been very happy in Harland County. She had friends there. Good friends. Ones that would never betray her. And...

Jace was in Harland County. At least, for a few more months.

Excitement quickened her pulse. If her mother didn't need help, and her brother didn't need to stay in the apartment, then she didn't need a better paying job after all. Didn't need to be in Colorado. She could continue to help her uncle, stay in the cute little cottage she'd grown to love, and be near her friends. Be there when Kerri had her baby. And Shayla had her baby. And Jace left for DWB.

Okay, that part sucked, but...he was still her friend, and she supported her friends, and she'd support him, especially with something that was so important to him.

"So, what do you say, Holly? You going to move to Texas, too?"

"Thinking about it." She blew out a breath and smiled. "I doubt I can get out of my lease. Not a whole seven months early. Not without having to pay a healthy penalty."

"If anyone can, you can."

"It's worth a try," her mother said. "And maybe you can do it next month like me."

She nodded. "Maybe."

The more she thought about it, the more she loved the idea of moving to Harland County. She could always make weekend trips to Colorado to ski. But, she'd grown to love the warmth she'd discovered in south Texas. And it had nothing to do with the climate, and everything to do with the people.

Especially a certain doctor.

It was the middle of December, and Jace was on his way to weekend drill. He'd picked Tanner up on his way into town, but only half-heard what his friend was saying, his mind was on the paperwork piled on his desk at work, paperwork piled on his desk at the armory, the upcoming holidays, family, and of course, Holly. He hadn't talked to her since before she'd left for Denver last month, but she was constantly on his mind.

Her uncle and Donny had been telling anyone who walked into The Creamery that she and her mother were moving to Harland County sometime this month. The news had helped make the past few weeks not suck so much. Looked like he might get that chance to fix the things his sister had mentioned at Thanksgiving.

"Holy shit! There's Holly," Tanner said, pointing to the woman lugging boxes into the little cottage.

Maybe even as soon as today.

Jace immediately slowed down, then pulled up next to her, his heart beats suddenly kicking the shit out of his ribs. "Text Kade. Tell him we'll be at the armory a few minutes late. We're going to help her unload."

Tanner nodded. "On it."

They got out of the truck and headed to her car as she walked out of the house and stopped dead. Then a big smile spread across her sweet lips, and it felt as if the sun had just come out from behind a cloud.

"Hey."

"Is that all you've got to say?" His buddy rushed forward to lift her up and spin her in a hug.

Her laughter filled the air and the sweet sound did something to his insides, but when Tanner placed her down and she transferred her attention to him, his damn boots were rooted to the pavement.

"It's good to see you," she said, her boots apparently not rooted, because she walked up to him, set her hands on his arms, and leaned in to kiss his cheek. "How've you been?"

The contact sent a jolt through his body, and just like that, he regained motor function again. He slid his hands up her arms and stared down into her pretty, flushed face. "Much better now."

She smiled and blushed a little more, and the two of them stood there next to her loaded car, hands on each other's arms, grinning at each other while Tanner snickered and stepped closer.

"Ah, hate to break up the…whatever it is, but these boxes aren't going to unload themselves."

"Yeah, right." He released her and spent the next ten minutes carrying her stuff inside.

"This all you have, Holly?" Tanner glanced around the pile of boxes they'd stacked in the middle of the living room.

She nodded. "Yep. I'd already unloaded my clothes before you arrived."

"No, I mean, no moving van or anything?"

"Oh, no." She shook her head. "After my landlord let me get out of my lease early, I spent the last two weeks selling all my furniture and things. It was quite liberating to purge unwanted items from your life, leaving you free to concentrate on what's important."

Her gaze had settled on Jace as she spoke, and he got the impression she was talking about a hell of a lot more than material possessions. Could he be one of the important things she wanted to concentrate on?

God, he hoped so.

"We'd better get going. It's great to have you back, Hol," Tanner said, kissing her cheek. "You're just in time for the McCalls' Christmas party tonight. Everyone's going to be so happy to see you again. We get out of drill at five. Wanna go to the McCalls' party?"

Jace had his mouth open, ready to ask, but his buddy beat him to it.

Holly hesitated, bouncing her gaze to him.

"I'm sure if you ask nicely, Jace will be happy to take you," his buddy told her.

She elbowed the snickering man, then turned back to face him.

He smiled and stepped right up to her. "I'd love to take you tonight."

Her green gaze heated, and his groin instantly sparked to life.

"I'd like that, too."

That hadn't been what he'd meant, but now that the thought was there, and her eyes were full of the smoldering taking place in his body, he wasn't going to be able to shake it. "Then I'll be back to pick you up at seven."

"I'll be ready," she replied with a grin.

An answering grin spread across his face, one he'd continued to wear the whole day and was still wearing as he pulled up in front of her cottage nearly twelve hours later.

When Holly opened the door on his second knock, his whole body tightened at the sight that greeted him.

"You look beautiful," he gushed, his chest tight and full with some unknown emotion as he stared at the beauty in a body-hugging, emerald green dress and high-heeled black boots that zipped up to her knees.

"Thanks." The color sweeping into her face only enhanced those gorgeous, fathomless eyes.

"Damn, Holly, I want to kiss you."

She sucked in a breath. "Why don't you?"

"Because I won't stop with just one, and we'd miss the party."

"Good."

He sucked in a breath this time and closed his eyes a moment, then reopened them. "No, it's not. That would be selfish. There are a lot of people who are going to want to see you. I've waited seven weeks to kiss you again, I can wait a little longer."

"Always thinking of others, Doc," she said, her gaze softening. "We'd better get going, then, because I'm not that thoughtful."

He knew that to be a bunch of bullshit, or she wouldn't have ushered him out the door.

Thirty-three minutes later, he didn't think he was going to make it. Just watching Holly laughing and hugging her friends, he was drawn in, mesmerized by her sweet, yet strong caring nature, and the way her expression radiated happiness.

He wanted to wrap his arms around her and soak it all in.

"Okay, so, I've been looking for someone to hand over my special holiday hat to, and well, I think one of you three would get the most use now that I no longer need it," Kevin said, walking up to him, Tanner, and Jesse where they stood having a beer with Kade.

In his hand was a great looking black Stetson, but the mistletoe fringe wasn't exactly Jace's style.

"Thanks, Kevin, but I think I'll pass," he said with a grin. He'd seen the cowboy put that thing into action way too many years. It had certainly gotten the attention of plenty of single women, but he wasn't interested in that.

He was only interested in one.

The grinning cowboy laughed. "Okay, Doc. I don't think you need it, anyway. Not with your gorgeous date batting her pretty green eyes at you."

Kevin pointed to Holly who was talking with his wife and a few other women in the corner. Her gaze lifted to him, and her smile widened.

His heart literally rocked into place.

"I'm going to pass, too, Kev." Tanner shrugged. "Not exactly my style."

"Mine either, but thanks," Jesse said.

Kade smirked. "Too bad Brandi's youngest brother wasn't here. I'm sure he'd be happy to carry on your tradition."

Kevin laughed. "Yeah. You're right. Maybe I'll ship it up to Keiffer. He's got what it takes to keep the tradition going."

"Speaking of traditions," Kade said, his gray gaze zeroing in on him. "I think you'd better hurry, Jace, or you're going to miss your window of opportunity." He motioned with his head in Holly's direction. "She's directly under the mistletoe Mrs. McCall has hanging near the window seat."

His pulse instantly kicked up as he spotted the decoration above her pretty head. "Excuse me," he said to his friends, never breaking eye contact with Holly as he strode straight to her. Being that they were in a room full of people, he was fairly certain he could contain the kiss to just one.

Maybe.

"Hi, Jace," Kerri said, followed by the other women, who spread apart, giving him straight access to his target.

Holly.

"Hello, ladies," he replied, still holding the excited green gaze. "Excuse me a moment. There's a bit of mistletoe tradition I need to take care of." Then he pulled Holly in close, his body thrilling at the feel of hers lined up and pressing against him, her warm hands gliding up his chest, over his shoulders to slide into his hair.

He curved one hand over her hip and cupped her head with the other before slowly lowering his mouth, hesitating a few breaths, amping up the anticipation until he could feel she'd stopped breathing.

Good, so had he.

Chapter Fifteen

Then he kissed her.

Holly's mouth parted, and then she was kissing him back.

Damn, he missed the feel of her, and her hot, sweet, hungry taste. He had to hold back a groan, vaguely remembering they were not alone. But, since they had an audience, he kept the kiss fun and flirty, brushing his tongue to hers before he pulled back.

"I...um…hello," she said, blinking up at him.

"Hello." His voice was a little rough. Probably because all the blood had drained out of his head. He noted the women smiling at them, and he felt compelled to say something. "If you'll excuse us, we're going to hit the dance floor."

He led Holly around a few guest to an opening where he pulled her in tight, amazed at how she fit like a perfect puzzle when she snuggled close and sighed. He felt himself relax for the first time in days…*weeks*.

Her fingers brushed the back of his neck, making him want to purr. She nudged closer, pressing against the zipper of his jeans that was growing tighter by the second.

"Mmm…you feel good," she murmured, then rocked again.

He stifled a groan and tightened his grip on her, thinking about letting his hands wonder over her back to cup her ass and haul her up tight. But since they weren't alone, he continued to behave.

"I'm beginning to think we should've stayed at my place," she said against his neck. "Do you think we've been at the party long enough?"

He drew back to stare into her face, his mind wanting to make sure he'd heard and understood what she was saying. Yep. He'd gotten the message correct. She wanted to be alone with him. Now.

That worked for Jace. "Yes, we've shown our faces. Let's leave. There are things I want to do to you that I can't do here."

Her smile grew wicked, and she leaned into him, the heat in her eyes turning him inside out and sideways. "I was just thinking the same. You see, I need a doctor. I'm experiencing some strange urges and cravings."

"Oh? Maybe you should describe your symptoms to me…slowly and in great detail."

And, son-of-a-bitch, she lifted up on her tiptoes, leaned in, her lips brushing his earlobe as she told him where she ached, how she ached, and asked if he'd use his healing hands on her to get rid of those aches.

He stilled, tightening his grip on her as he sucked in a breath. "Yeah, I can fix that," he croaked, his throat tight…like his jeans.

Jace took her hand and tugged her off the floor. He had several weeks of pent up, sexual energy rushing through his body, ruling his actions.

Holly laughed as her booted heels clip-clopped at a fast rate as she tried to keep up with him. "On a mission, are you, Doc?"

He glanced over his shoulder at her, letting his gaze tell her what she wanted to know. She blinked, and her amusement turned to anticipation darkening her gaze.

Shit. She had him so hard he throbbed. He shot his gaze around the immediately area as he looked for somewhere more secluded, because there was no way in hell he'd make it to her cottage right now.

They'd just stepped passed the buffet when his phone began to ring. He stiffened and stopped dead. She halted at his side and tugged free.

Ah, hell.

"You'd better get it."

He didn't want to. For the first time in his life, he didn't want to be a doctor. He just wanted a small break. An hour. He'd take a half-hour, even. But, that wasn't part of the Hippocratic Oath he'd taken. So, he reluctantly released her to answer his phone.

Five minutes later, after Kevin and Shayla assured they'd take Holly home, he was on his way to the hospital to meet up with the ambulance bringing in one of his patients. He was going to have to *diagnose* Holly's symptoms another time.

Three days since the Christmas party, and Holly had yet to *play doctor* with Jace. As usual, his life was hectic. So far, they'd managed one shared smoothie at The Creamery on Sunday when he'd stopped in after drill on his way to the hospital to check on his patient admitted to ICU after suffering a massive heart attack Saturday, and a quick lunch at his office yesterday—minus the mind blowing orgasm. Poor guy kept apologizing, but she really did understand. He had a good heart. His patients were his friends. And she would not want to see him change any of it.

She was willing to work her life around his, something she never, ever considered doing before. But Jace was special, and she was happy to share whatever time she could with him. He'd called her before and told her that maybe they'd be able to fit some time in tomorrow night, so when she opened the door to his knock two hours later, she didn't mask her surprise.

"Jace! Come on in. I think you're a day early…" Her voice trailed off as her mind registered the bleak, hollow look in his eyes while she shut the door behind him. "What is it?" she reached up to touch his face.

He blinked, and stared down at her as if he wasn't sure how he'd gotten there. "We lost Mr. Samuels today. He had another heart attack…"

What she heard in his tone was that *he* lost Mr. Samuels. The doctor obviously felt responsible for the death. She was smart enough to recognize words wouldn't help, so she stepped close, wrapped her arms around him and rested her head on his chest.

After a brief moment, his strong arms clamped around her, and he held her tight. Real tight. His heart rocked a little underneath her ear, then leveled off to a strong, steady beat. She wasn't sure how long they stood there, perfectly content to let him hold on as long as he needed.

When he finally loosed his hold and stepped back, he was still pale and his gaze was full of shadows. "I'm sorry. I should go," he said turning for her door.

"Oh no. You don't need to be alone tonight, Jace. Stay here."

He shook his head. "Thanks, but I'm not that good of company right now."

And before she could stop him, he left.

Unsure what to do, she paced, hoping the movement would clear her mind. She didn't think he went home, since his truck had taken off in the opposite direction.

Damn.

She wasn't good at this. Her heart ached for the guy. She wanted to make it all better, but had no damn idea how.

She was still fighting an inner battle an hour later when there was another knock on the door. It was Jace. And Kade.

More specific, Kade helping a slightly inebriated Jace into her cottage.

"Bastard. I told you to take me home," the doctor grumbled, aggravation mixing with the sadness in his blue eyes.

"No can do, buddy. There's no one else at your house, and I didn't figure you wanted me to drop you on your mother's porch."

"Hell no."

"Then have a seat, man," Kade said, giving the doctor a small push that sent his friend onto the couch. "Today is not a day to be alone."

"That's what I told him before he left an hour ago."

Jace muttered a curse. "I don't need you to worry about my sorry ass."

"Too late."

A slight smile tugged at Kade's mouth as he motioned for her to meet him at the door. "Kerri called me, said he was in the booth in the back of the kitchen at her restaurant, nursing a bottle of scotch. So, I came down and had a beer with him, then persuaded him to leave the Pub and the bottle. I don't want him to be alone, and since he doesn't invite women to his house, I took a gamble that you wouldn't mind if I brought him here. But if you'd prefer, I can take him back to my ranch."

She immediately shook her head. "No. Thanks for bringing him back. I was going crazy trying to figure out where he'd gone after telling me about Mr. Samuels."

The cowboy nodded, a few shadows crossing into his gray eyes. "He takes it personal. When we lost Sergeant Nylon during deployment last year, I had to pull him away. He'd been working on the kid for over two hours...*after* Bobby had flat-lined. There hadn't been much to work on to begin with." He shook his head as if trying to dispel the horrific images in his mind. "In case you hadn't noticed, Jace has a hard time giving up on people."

Wasn't that the truth?

And her heart squeezed so tight with all his friend had just revealed about him, she hurt every time she tried to draw in air.

"I won't let him leave again tonight," she vowed.

He nodded. "Don't hesitate to call if he gives you trouble." Then the caring man dropped Jace's keys into her hand and left.

She glanced at the couch. Jace was leaning back, eyes closed, a disgusted expression pinching his face. Quickly stashing the keys in a cupboard, she kept him in her line of sight, her chest still tight.

Tears and pity would not help, so she sucked it up and headed back toward him. "Jace, can I get you something to eat?"

"Not hungry. Thanks," he said, then opened his eyes. "It's late. Why don't you just go to bed. I'll be all right here on the couch."

"You're right. It is late," she said, reaching for his hands and tugging him to his feet. He was drunk, but still coherent. "Come on. Into bed with you."

He didn't object when she slid her arm around his waist and helped him into her bedroom.

"Are you leading me in here to have your way with me?"

She laughed. "No." Then twisted them, before palming his chest and pushing him onto the bed.

He lifted up onto his elbows and stared at her. "You sure? Because it feels as if you are."

Holly dropped to her knees and, ignoring his groan, began to remove his shoes, then socks.

"Still feels like it."

A smile tugged her lips, but she remained quiet when he unhooked his jeans and pushed them to his knees. She grabbed the cuffs and yanked.

"This isn't a good idea," he said, when she leaned over him to remove his shirt.

But again, he didn't protest. She shut off the lights.

"Definitely feels like it," he said.

She laughed and quickly changed into her nightshirt, then crawled into bed with him. "Come here," she said, tugging him up to the pillows, then under the covers.

"Aren't you supposed to be naked?" he asked, curling her into his side.

Holly slid her hand up his chest. "Not tonight."

"Headache?" he asked, his big hand gliding up her body to settle on her forehead. "You don't have a fever."

The way his palm just brushed over her nipples and the other cupped her ass, yeah, she most definitely had a fever. But the timing was wrong.

"This isn't about me, Jace. It's about you. Let me help you. Tell me what you need."

He tried to move her, but she pushed back. "I need to go—"

"No, you need to let me take care of you." She eased her grip and lightly trailed her fingers into his hair. "You don't need to be alone tonight."

"I don't need to talk, either."

"Might help if you did," she said.

"No. What's done is done. Once again, I wasn't…" His voice trailed off, leaving his analogy unspoken, and her throat hot with unshed tears.

"This was not your fault, Jace."

"Then whose was it, Holly? I was his doctor."

"Yes, a doctor who did all he could for a seventy-eight-year-old man with a history of heart disease and heart attacks."

He stiffened. "How'd you know?"

"Tanner," she replied.

"Figures," he mumbled, trying to get up again.

She held fast. "When you left before, I called around looking for you. Tanner told me Mr. Samuel's history."

A second later, she found herself under Jace, pinned by his hot, solid, body. "I'm thinking maybe we should stop talking now."

"Okay," she said, wiggling until he was half-on and half-off her body. "Let me hold you."

His scotch-tainted breath was warm on her skin while she ran her fingers through his hair, and gently stroked up and down his arm with the other.

"Still feels like it," he mumbled against her neck, just before he fell asleep.

Jace woke the next morning remembering only bits and pieces of the night before, and damn glad Holly wasn't next to him in bed. He got out, then winced as the room spun, and a piercing pain shot through his head.

Good. Served him right for being so stupid.

When his eyes were able to refocus, he spied the note Holly left him on a pillow. A small grin twitched his lips as he lifted the peach paper which told him his keys were on the counter, truck was across the street at the Pub, and to be careful.

He fished his phone out of his pocket and called her.

She answered on the first ring. “Hey, you okay?”

“Fabulous,” he lied, smiling when her soft chuckle echoed in his ear.

“That good, huh? There’s pills in the medicine cabinet. Help yourself.”

He headed for the bathroom, rubbing his temple in an attempt to lessen the ache. “Thanks, Holly.” If he never saw another bottle of scotch, it would be too soon.

“Any time,” she said.

The woman was too sweet. He downed the pills before returning to the bedroom, biting back a curse when he noticed the time.

“Sorry I had to leave, but Donny ended up in the emergency room this morning.”

He stilled. “Jesus, is he okay?”

“Yeah, three stitches in his head. Said he had a fight with a vacuum cleaner and lost. And don’t worry, it wasn’t here. It happened at home.”

At least she didn’t have to deal with a workman’s comp claim.

“Why don’t you stop by? I’ll make you a banana smoothie.”

“Deal. Give me ten minutes.” he told her then hung up.

He was ready in five.

And when he walked inside her shop and found her alone, he strode straight to her, pulled her close, and kissed her.

She melted against him, slipping her arms around his neck and snuggling close. He'd planned to give her a simple thank you kiss, but it got a little out of control, and soon their hands were all over, sneaking under clothes, caressing hot skin.

When they broke for air, he set his forehead on hers and squeezed her shoulders. "Damn, you're potent."

"Ditto."

He nodded, holding her a moment while he got his hunger under control. "Thanks for last night," he said, drawing back to lightly trace her jaw. "I'm really sorry you had to deal with my drunk ass. And I'm sorry I fell asleep, it wasn't my intention."

"I know." Her lips curved into a smile. "It was mine."

He narrowed his gaze, pretending to be hurt. "What happened to discussing symptoms with me?"

She laughed, pushing out of his arms to grab a smoothie from the counter. "That is saved for another appointment."

"What appointment?"

"I don't know. I'll have to pencil it in."

He nodded. "Sorry, my schedule gets a bit crazy some weeks."

"No worries. I can wait," she said softly.

He groaned, wanting very much to put a closed sign on the door, lock it, and put an end to their waiting.

"Hey, Jace. Holly." Connor strode into the shop. "How's things?"

She stepped around him to greet her customer. "Good. How's Kerri? She's heading into her final trimester, right?"

"Yeah, thankfully. It'll be nice when these cravings stop."

Holly nodded, but he didn't think she knew the man wasn't just talking about his wife.

"I've got your order right here." Pushing a white bag filled with who knows what, and a cup holder with two milkshakes at the tall cowboy, she smiled. "You're all set."

"Thanks." Conner dropped some cash near the register, then turned and rushed out the door.

Seemed more like coffee and hot chocolate season than milkshakes to Jace, but he figured it had something to do with his friend's unwanted cravings.

Hiding a smile, he came around in front of the display case, deliberately putting a very large, inanimate object between them. "Well, I better go. Need to run home to shower and change before work." He pushed back from the counter. "Listen, I already know tonight and tomorrow are nuts, but how about Friday? Are you working Friday evening?"

"No."

He leaned back toward her. "Want to come to my place for dinner?"

"Your place?"

"Yeah."

Her gaze softened as she stared at him. "I'd like that."

"Good." He smiled, heart thudding hard in his chest. "I'll see you around seven?"

She nodded, gaze warm and soft, nearly making him forget he was going to be late for work if he didn't hurry. "See you then."

And he would. He planned to see all of her then. See and touch and kiss and lick and take care of all her symptoms. Twice.

What she'd done last night blew his mind. He'd never known a woman who would put up with him like she had as he dealt with a loss. Most women shied away and left him to deal with things on his own. That's how he thought it was supposed to be. Until Holly.

Last night, yeah, he was drunk, but he remembered everything, especially how she didn't crowd him with pity, spouting useless niceties, or tell him to grow a pair. No. She'd wrapped her arms around him and shared her heart and her strength. And God, he'd needed them both.

Feared he'd always need them.

He didn't know if that was in the cards, but he did know he wanted to browse the deck and find out.

Friday night, he planned to spread the cards and see.

Chapter Sixteen

When Friday evening rolled around, Holly was more than ready to see Jace again. It'd only been a day and a half, but it was strange; it'd felt like days. Years.

Since the temperature had dropped, she'd nixed her plans to wear a dress. Opting for jeans, boots, and a sweater. And if she played her cards right, she wouldn't be wearing them most of the night, anyway.

She turned into the long drive, and continued past trees and pastures and fields, then pulled into the driveway in front of Jace's brick house. Her heart beats elevated, and her hand shook as she knocked on his red door, made more vibrant by the setting sun.

She couldn't believe she was there. That he'd invited her to his house. She knew this was not only big in their relationship, it was a big step for Jace.

The door opened, and her greeting dissipated at the sight of him in a pair of jeans and charcoal gray Henley, his hair still damp from a recent shower.

"Hi. Come on in. It's getting cold out," he said and tugged her inside.

The place was inviting and warm with the living room wide-open to the modern kitchen with high cabinets, granite counters, and matching backsplash. The stools at the breakfast bar matched the loveseat and couch facing the fireplace. But the best part was the gorgeous wood trim and floors, and spectacular, high wood-beamed ceilings. It reminded her a little of Colorado, and felt like…home.

"Wow. This place is…wow," she repeated, allowing him to help her out of her black leather jacket.

Walking into the kitchen, he set it on the back of one of the chairs and pointed to the set table. "Would you like a glass of wine?"

She nodded, and because watching the man made her insides smolder, she turned around to take in the view of his living room. Tastefully done in masculine colors, but with just the right amount of warmth, the room had a pleasant, relaxing feel. Exactly what the busy doctor would need when he got home from his hectic days. The stone fireplace, complete with roaring fire, caught and held her attention, until she spied an undecorated, live Christmas tree in a stand in front of his large window.

"You have a tree," she said inanely.

He nodded, stepping near to hand her a glass. "I was kind of hoping you'd help me decorate it this weekend."

Of all the things he could've said, that was not at all what she'd expected. A sharp thrill shot through Holly, adding to the warmth his friendly gaze had started the instant he'd answered her knock.

"I'd love to." She sipped her wine for something to do to keep her hands and mouth occupied.

"Dinner is ready. We can move it here if you'd like." He motioned to the coffee table near the fireplace. The setting was damn near perfect, but also in plain view of the kitchen table.

"Since the table is already set, I'm okay with having it there," she told him. "It smells wonderful, by the way."

A sheepish grin curved his lips as he set a hand at the small of her back and ushered her toward the food.

"It should. Kerri cooked it. She left about ten minutes ago."

She chuckled. "No wonder it smells so great."

Taking the seat he pulled out for her, she nodded her thanks, and talked her body into dealing with one hunger at a time. And damn, the man looked good enough to eat, sitting across from her, gaze all open and warm.

"Thanks for coming," he said.

She must've had a few too many sips of wine on her empty stomach, because she nearly blurted out, *Not yet*.

"Thanks for inviting me."

They smiled at each other a few seconds, and when the air began to change between them, he cleared his throat and motioned for her to eat. Happy for the distraction, she loaded her plate with a little of each dish Kerri had made, knowing she'd enjoy every bite of chicken cordon bleu, green beans almandine, rice pilaf and tomato aspic with shrimp salad.

Thirty-minutes later, she sat next to him on the floor, on a lush, area rug in front of the fire with the rest of the wine, one hunger satisfied and the other burning out of control.

"I've thought about bringing you here. A lot, Holly," he said, taking her half-empty glass and setting it by his on the coffee table behind them. "I thought about you naked, and me buried deep inside you."

"Oh," she whispered, anticipation trembling inside her.

He lifted a hand to cup her face and lean close. "My phone is off and in the back room. We're not going to be interrupted again."

She smiled her approval.

"Where's your phone?"

"I left it home."

"Clever girl," he said against her lips, nibbling softly, then leaning forward, pressing her down onto the carpet.

Before she could blink, he was on her, spark ignited at the McCalls' party blazing back to life. "It's been too long, Holly. I'm not going to be able to go slow this first time. Sorry."

With his mouth on hers, he slid his hands beneath her shirt, grazing her skin, sending shivers down her body. The fact he'd said the *first* time wasn't lost on her, despite the desire fogging her brain. She was thrilled to hear there'd be more than one time.

His thumbs brushed over her nipples, and she gasped. He was taking her apart. Between his touch and his hunger, she was on board with anything he wanted.

"We need to lose the clothes." He pulled back and slowly peeled her sweater over her head, before yanking off his Henley.

She couldn't take her gaze off him. Muscles rippled as he bent to kiss her breast that spilled from her bra, and then suddenly that lace barrier was gone.

"Been thinking of this," he murmured against her peak, flicking the nipple with his tongue before sucking it hard into his mouth.

Her gasped echoed through the room as she writhed beneath him.

"You're so damn soft."

His voice was deliciously low and sexy, and she nearly came from the sound of him alone. Then he slid the tips of his fingers into her jeans, upping the tension to insane.

"Jace," she whispered.

"I know." His blue gaze was dark and very, very hot. He grasped her hand and placed it over his erection. “No more talking. I have plans for our mouths.” To prove it, he sat back and tugged her jeans off before he removed his.

Perfect, sinewy, and hot, his body gleamed in the firelight, and her breath caught at the sight of every inch of his mouthwatering form. And he had a lot of mouthwatering inches.

He crawled up her body and bent to kiss her, low on her quivering stomach as he snagged her panties with his fingers and slowly tugged them down. “You’re so beautiful, Holly.” He settled between her thighs, taking so long to look his fill, she squirmed.

“Jace.”

“So damn beautiful.”

He nudged her legs open with his broad shoulders and bent to kiss an inner thigh. Her pulse raced, her body wanting…*needing* him to give her more. Then he gently stroked her with his thumb before he groaned and ran his tongue over her. Holly’s mind blanked. She bit her lip and cupped his head, unable to stop from bucking.

“Damn, you taste good,” he murmured, and when her hips rocked again, he slid his hands beneath her, holding her still for his care and attention. “I’m going to make you scream.”

Surprised by her body’s quick reaction, she trembled, hovering on the very edge of an orgasm. Already.

He laved his tongue where her leg met her body, taking his time while she shifted, trying to get him where she wanted him most.

“Good?”

“Y—*yes*.”

He brushed his lips over her center, then did it again. This time, he slid one finger into her, and then another, with long, slow, sure strokes.

Her breath hitched, and when he gently closed his teeth on her, she lifted up. “Jace…*please*…”

“Whatever you need,” he promised before he sucked her into his mouth.

She screamed, in a low, lengthy moan as she came. He’d warned her he was going to make her scream, and he did. Still holding onto his head, she tangled her fingers in his hair, shuddering endlessly beneath him. He stayed with her all the way through, and when she finally went limp, he kissed a slow path up her still-quivering body. His lips were hot and hungry when they finally met hers, and she tightened her hold, feeling him hard and throbbing near her hip.

“Please, Jace. I need you inside me.”

He sat back, and fished a condom from his jeans, his arousal proud and thick. Watching him roll the condom down his length made her insides clench. He entwined their fingers and brought their joined hands to rest on either side of her face. She held his gaze, watching the deep blue darken to near black as he nudged the tip between her thighs before sliding into her. Another deep moan ripped up her throat. He felt so good filling her. Giving her everything.

The man always gave her everything.

“Damn, Holly.”

She wanted to give him everything, too. Wrapping her legs around his hips, she arched up and felt him slip farther inside.

“So perfect,” he whispered hoarsely, squeezing their entwined fingers.

When she was with him like this, open, vulnerable, trusting, she felt wanted and beautiful, and completely connected on much more than a physical level.

Then he was moving, setting a pace that stole her breath and captured her thudding heart. She freed her hands to cup his face, holding his gaze, knowing her own was filled with awe and wonder.

Was this what it felt like when it was right?

Jace slid his hands beneath her, sliding them up her back to grip her shoulders. The movement pulled them closer, pushing him deeper inside her, and she let out a hungry, needy sound, quivering in pure pleasure. As her eyes started to drift closed, he tangled a hand in her hair and gently tugged until she opened them again. His delicious, smoldering gaze held hers, allowing her to see his wants and fears and joy, allowing him the same as she shuddered and trembled and came, taking him with her over the edge for the blissful journey.

She was treading new territory, and got the impression it was the same for him. It scared her to be so open and trusting. This man had the ability to crush her heart, but he also had the ability to give it wings.

It was the middle of January, and Jace was in the middle of a normal week, in the middle of a normal day filled with the normal round of patients and their problems. Yet, his mind kept straying to Holly. There was nothing normal about the incredible woman, but he couldn't keep thinking that at the moment because of his patients. He'd already treated several cases of strep throat, two flus, one stitch job, and now Connor.

"You've got to stop this, Doc." The tall cowboy paced back and forth, his lanky body only needing two strides.

Jace leaned his back against the counter and waited for the man to stop.

"Seriously. Jelly donuts and cheese whip?" He halted, face twisting to match the disgust in his dark eyes. "I don't even like cheese whip."

"It will stop. In about three months. Hang in there. You're doing great."

"Great? How can you say that? I've even gained five pounds!"

If the cowboy didn't have such a physically demanding job, Jace feared the weight gain would've been four times greater. He decided to keep that observation to himself. The poor father-to-be was stressed enough.

"There's got to be something I can take."

He shook his head. "Sorry. There isn't anything I can give you for cravings. I can only suggest something for the heartburn or upset stomach caused by your food combinations."

"That's just it. There aren't any. Just more damn cravings."

"Well, have you tried mind over matter? Maybe reaching for a stalk of celery instead of the donut?"

To his surprise, the cowboy nodded.

"Yeah, but it didn't taste nearly as good as the donut."

Jace bit the inside of his lip. *Don't laugh. Do not laugh.* None of his patients had ever tested his resolve to remain professional. Just Connor.

He decided to switch gears. Try changing the man's focus.

"How's Kerri?"

"She's good. Doesn't have a craving for cheese whip."

He resisted the urge to swipe a hand over his face. "Have you started working on the nursery?"

"Yeah. We met with Brandi last week to discuss transforming Kerri's old room, now that we know we're having a girl." The big guy's face softened.

Smiling, he stepped forward and thrust out his hand. "Congratulations, Connor. That's wonderful."

"Thanks. And we heard Shayla found out yesterday that she's having one, too, so who knows? Maybe they'll grow up to be best friends."

Jace nodded, happy that some of his friends had settled down and were building families and futures. Someday, maybe that would be him.

An image of Holly smiling lovingly down into the face of their newborn flashed through his mind. His heart rocked, cracking open, sending a strange warmth through his body. He leaned heavily back against the counter and blinked.

He loved the thought of her carrying his child. It should've scared the shit out of him, but instead, he felt strangely…whole.

"So, what about you, Jace?"

He blinked, refocusing on his patient. "What?"

"You and Holly? You've been a lot closer since she returned."

He nodded, but was ready to change the subject back to cravings if he had to.

"Good for you. She's a good woman."

Again, he nodded.

"She goes the extra mile to help people out."

It was one of the things he loved most about her.

Jace's heart rocked hard against his ribs as that thought sunk in.

He *loved* Holly.

How the hell had that happened?

By the time February rolled around, Holly had to admit, she'd never been happier. All thanks to her uncle having surgery and her making the best decision ever to go to Texas and help him out. She'd met great friends, enjoyed her job, had less stress. Even took a night course in photography offered at the local college Caitlin and Donny attended.

All wonderful reasons for her happy state of mind, but not the main one. No. That honor was reserved for one hardworking, giving, handsome as hell doctor.

A doctor.

Never had she ever thought she'd get involved with another doctor again. And yet, Jace was unlike the other's she knew. He cared about his patients and people and family more than money or what was in it for him.

It was one of the things she loved most about him.

And she did love him.

She'd accepted that weeks ago. But the man would be leaving within two months. So, now she had to decide whether to tell him or not.

Same went for the phone call she'd received an hour ago from her old job back in Colorado. Her replacement hadn't worked out. They wanted her back.

"Oh my gosh! Little pink cowgirl boots. Thanks, Jordan! These are adorable," Kerri gushed, sitting next to Shayla in the middle of the Dalton's living room as the two expectant mothers opened gifts at their combined baby shower.

Her dilemma with Jace would have to wait. Now was the time to celebrate the upcoming births of two very lucky little girls.

"You're welcome, sis. My niece is going to be stepping out in style," Jordan said, sitting next to Holly.

Shayla opened her gift to reveal a matching pair.

"And so will her friend." The sheriff winked.

"Thanks, Jordan." The redhead laughed. "Your sister and I are going to have the best dressed kids in the county."

"And most spoiled," Kerri added.

Laughter went up around the room, and the next two hours flew by as Holly enjoyed being included in the happy occasion. The Daltons and McCalls had made her, and her mother's, transition to Texas effortless. They welcomed them into their families with open arms, and the only other place she'd felt more content was in a certain doctor's arms.

And she was itching to fast-forward the day so she could get to the point where they were both naked and spent.

"I recognize that dreamy look. You're in love with Jace Turner," Jordan said as they finished cleaning up after the party. "I'm happy for you. Jace is a great man. You two are good for each other."

"Thanks." She smiled, not shying away from the enveloping warmth brought on by her friend's statement, or denying it. Besides, the woman was too astute to be bullshitted.

"If you need to talk or cry or beat the shit out of something when he leaves for DWB, let me know. I have a heavy bag set up in the back room at the precinct."

Her lips quivered in an effort to keep the smile in place, even though her insides felt as if they'd become a heavy bag. She'd always known he was leaving. Knew the day would come. She just never realize how much it would hurt. But, it didn't matter. The thought of him doing what he loved, what he'd always planned, and all the lives he was about to touch, filled her with such a comforting warmth, all her pain minimized to a manageable ache.

"I'll keep it in mind," she replied. "Probably try a pint of Death-By-Chocolate first, though."

Her friend laughed. "Good call. Just remember, my offer still stands if you need to work off the calories consumed."

This time, Holly laughed and was still smiling as she made her way across Shadow Rock to the new shelter where Jace and the guys were volunteering while their women were busy with the baby shower.

Anticipation of their night ahead upped her pace. They were spending it his place again. His invitation into his home back in December had turned their fun into a relationship, and although it scared her to be so open, she'd never felt more connected and loved. Neither of them had said the words yet, and more than likely for the same reason. They didn't want to scare the other off.

Well, it would take a hell of a lot more than that to scare her, and she was figuring that maybe he felt the same way. Maybe tonight, she'd finally say it out loud.

"So, Jace. You're coming down the home stretch, buddy." Connor's voice drifted out to her through the opened door.

"Yeah, you're really going to resign your commission this month?" Kade asked.

"Not sure," he replied, stopping her in her tracks.

What?

"Having second thoughts about the DWB?" Kade asked.

"I'm betting its second thoughts about leaving Holly."

Someone snickered.

Her heart squeezed. And she figured it served her right for eaves dropping. She was probably going to go to hell.

"Connor's right. I'm not sure I want to go anymore."

Half of her heart rejoiced, but the other half-squeezed so tight she had to rub her chest to ease the ache.

"You're in love with her," Kade stated.

"That's great," Connor said, and she could hear a round of backslapping echoing in the air.

"Yeah, trouble is, I've no idea what to do about it."

She knew.

She knew exactly what to do.

And her heart sank.

No way was Jace staying. He had to join Doctors Without Borders. It was his life's dream. His dad's, too, no doubt. She couldn't be—*wouldn't be*—the one to stand in the way of that dream, or stop him from caring for all those people he was going to touch.

God, she wanted to. She loved him, didn't want to let him go.

But, because she loved him, she *had* to let him go. Because he was about to make the biggest mistake of his life, and she didn't want to be the cause of his biggest regret by making him stay. She just couldn't do that. Couldn't be that selfish.

Chapter Seventeen

As quietly as possible, Holly retraced her steps, and sat on the porch, talking her heart into not shattering. Jordan came out a few minutes later, took one look at her and frowned.

"What's going on?"

Sucking it up, she stood and strode to the woman. "I need a ride home."

The sheriff cocked her head and narrowed her eyes on her, then transferred her gaze to the shelter before settling back on her. "Jace?"

She shook her head. "I need to think. Can't do that with him around."

"Okay," Jordan said, apparently mulling it over and finding her excuse acceptable. "Come on. I'm heading to the precinct near your cottage anyway."

Although they drove in silence for several minutes, she could hear the wheels turning in her friend's head and wasn't surprised when she finally spoke.

"You do know running away from a problem doesn't help."

Holly nodded. "I'm not running. In fact, I'm going to offer him a solution. He's just not going to be happy at first."

"I'm not sure I like the sound of this." A deep frown creased Jordan's brow as she pulled up outside the cottage. "What are you planning?"

"It's okay," she assured, fighting back the sting of tears. "You sacrifice for those you love, right?"

"Always."

"Then I'm going to help him make the right decision."

A sense of doom settled over Jace's chest and squeezed as he drove to Holly's. Why would she just leave like that? They'd had plans. She knew they'd had plans. So, when he'd finished at the shelter and strode up to the house to find she'd left with Jordan, he knew something was wrong.

A quick call to the sheriff had confirmed it. Oh, Jordan didn't tell him much. No, that wasn't the woman's style, but she did tell him Holly had said she had a decision to make.

Decision? What damn decision?

He was contemplating it as he parked in front of her place and knocked on her door. Phone to her ear, she opened it and stepped back to let him in. As he entered, that ball of doom lodged in his chest grew.

"Okay," she said into the phone. "I will. Thanks for calling."

"What's going on, Holly? Why'd you leave?" He stepped close and lifted a hand to touch her arm, but she moved back. "Holly?"

"That was work. Colorado work. They're offering me my old job back."

Not at all what he'd expected. "Oh." He sat on the nearest chair because his legs suddenly felt as if they'd been knocked out from under him. "Are you going to take it?"

She nodded. "I just did."

He didn't know what hurt worse, the fact she was going to move back to Colorado, or the fact she hadn't even thought to talk it over with him.

Both.

"I see."

"It's great, isn't it? You're about to leave the country for a new job, and I'll be heading back home for mine."

"Yeah, great," he said, as if on auto pilot. "I'm not sure I want you to go."

She blinked and opened her mouth, but nothing came out. He understood her shock. He was a bit surprised he'd let that slip, then a little mad that she'd think he wouldn't care.

He rose to his feet and faced her. "I guess it was my mistake for assuming I meant a little more to you."

She closed her mouth and nodded.

The pain he'd felt before was nothing to the crushing weight gripping his chest at her admission.

"I'm sorry, Jace. But we never talked about it being more than great sex."

Since that was true, he decided he had no reason to hold it against her. Not once had he brought up the subject of a relationship, just foolishly assumed they'd both been on the same page. Wanting the same things. Feeling the same things. Hell, he'd never even told her he loved her. How could he expect her to think what they were doing was more than just great sex?

"When do you leave?" he finally asked.

Her head lifted slightly. "Three weeks. Well, I start then. I told them I had to wait until Uncle Arthur finds a replacement. That'll give me one week to find a place to live and move back."

"Seems like you've got it all figure out, so I'd better let you get to it," he said, turning to walk toward the door.

"I'm sorry, Jace," she said, but made no move to stop him.

Or fix his heart. Remove the invisible blade skewering him alive.

He turned to look at her one last time. "Yeah, me, too." Then he let himself out of her house.

Out of her life.

The news of Holly leaving spread through Harland County faster than a summer downdraft. She dealt with daily well-wishers, and hugs, and tears, some of them her own, but she was determined not to crack.

You're doing this for Jace.

Several times a day, she chanted that reminder and drew strength from an image she'd created in her mind of the handsome doctor leaning over a child in an impoverished county, administering his own brand of healing.

She knew in her heart that was where he belonged. That was his calling. As much as she loved him, and hated that she was hurting him, her heart and mind told her she was doing the right thing.

"I hope you know what you're doing, Hol," Tanner said, later that afternoon as they spent her last day paddle boarding.

So do I.

"I'm a pro now at paddle boarding," she replied, knowing that wasn't what he'd meant.

Gliding on the lake next to her, he sent her a grouchy scoff. "I'm talking about Jace. You're breaking the guy's heart. And you're breaking yours. So, what gives? Why are you leaving?"

"We've been through this."

"Yep. And even after the six times you've recited the same verbiage, it still makes no damn sense," he said, maneuvering to the shore and stepping off with ease.

She mimicked his movements, then grabbed her gear and strode up the shore.

"Not answering speaks volumes, you know, Hol."

She eye-rolled him, but remained silent as they turned in their paddles and boards to the rental shack. Her heart caught at the realization she wasn't going to be around for the upcoming busy season.

Colorado had its own busy season. How the hell could she forget that?

Oh, right, because her heart hurt so damn bad her soul reeled, and her mind had to deal with the fall out.

"Okay, so the silence isn't working, Holly." Tanner took her by the hand and led her to a bench and sat. "Let's have it. Spill."

She decided it was a good opportunity to gain information she needed. "Did Jace leave the guard?"

"Yep. He resigned his commission last week," he answered, sadness clouding his gaze. "Won't be the same without him there."

"Did he join DWB?"

"Yep, same day he resigned. He leaves in eighteen days." Another sad shake of his head. "Harland won't be the same without him either."

She nodded, then stood, suddenly feeling oddly relieved. Doctor Jace Turner was now a part of Doctors Without Borders. Overjoyed, she hugged Tanner and sighed.

"That's great news."

He drew back and frowned down at her. "What? That he's leaving? Or that I'm bummed?"

Laughing, she patted his face. "You'll survive. I'm sure you'll find a nice blonde…or three, to help you with that."

"I think you're confusing me with Kevin."

"Nope, but that Casanova does give me hope that you'll find someone and settle down."

He snorted. "Wow, now you're reaching."

"Uh-huh."

He pulled them to their feet and dropped an arm around her shoulders as they walked to the parking lot. "And I also know what you're doing. Trying to change the focus of our conversation."

"Yep. And it worked." She chuckled, stopping at her car. "I've got to get back. Kerri's cooking a farewell dinner at the Texas Republic for me tonight."

A ripple of something flickered through his eyes then disappeared so fast she wondered if maybe she'd imagined it. "Yeah, I know. I'll see you there. So will half the county."

Her heart rolled. "Shoot. I didn't want anything big. Just wanted to have dinner with my friends."

"Like I said, half the county will be there," he said, pulling her in for another hug. "When are you leaving tomorrow?"

"Six in the morning. Lots of miles to cover the next two days."

He nodded and drew back. "Shoot me a text when you stop for the night."

"Yes, Mom."

He laughed, kissed her cheek, then stood back so she could get in her car. She was going to miss Tanner. He was a kindred spirit. Okay, a bit more wild than hers, but they'd connected, too. She'd already made tentative plans to have him visit in November to hit the slopes.

As she pulled out of the parking lot, she heaved a sigh. Things were looking up. Things were good. Jace hadn't shucked his dreams for her. He was going to accomplish his goal, and even though it meant she'd never see him again, she'd always know he was happy. And that was enough. It would have to be.

Jace was miserable.

He'd left his practice, left the guard, and would soon be leaving the states to travel and help the less fortunate around the world. All things he'd wanted, strove for, dreamt about his whole life.

And yet, he was miserable.

He tried to find that happy rush thinking about DWB always produced, but ever since Holly told him she was going back to Colorado, he seemed to have misplaced his happy. *Ah, hell.* He sounded like a dweeb.

Exercising Beckham, he rode the horse long and hard, trying to exercise his own stress away. Wasn't working. He dismounted and led the steed around the stables to hose him off and rub him down, his brisk movements helping with some of that stress, and apparently pleasing the horse who neighed his approval.

"Wow, can't believe Lacey let you near her baby," Tanner said, strolling into the barn.

"I thought I heard your bike. What's up?" he asked, continuing his task without making eye contact.

A mistake he knew not to make with the guy. Tanner had the same eerie inner bullshit meter reader as Kade and Jordan. Lethal when you didn't want to talk about your problems.

Kade had already put him through the ringer last week. Okay, not fair. He knew his friend was just worried about him. The guy didn't tolerate bullshit. He made you identify your problem and deal with it head on.

Jace knew what his problem was…Holly. And the fact he'd fallen for her, and she hadn't fallen back. Not much he could do about it now. Especially since she'd be in another state in less than twenty-four hours, and he'd be in another country in less than three weeks.

"Came to talk to you about Holly."

He stilled for a second, then led the horse to his stall. "Done talking about her, Tanner."

"No, I mean I just spent the day paddle boarding with her and learned something interesting I thought you'd like to know," the man claimed, following him down the stable.

"Tanner, I—"

"About the *real* reason she's leaving. And it's not work up in Colorado."

This got his attention. He secured the horse in his stall, then slowly turned to face his grinning buddy. "What are you talking about?"

"You." The guy rocked back on his heels, smug expression pulling his mouth into a face-consuming grin.

"Me?"

"Yep. Now, I'll admit she wouldn't answer any of my questions directly, but you know I can read people, and I was reading her loud and clear."

"I'm listening." And he was barely breathing, too. Not with his heart lodged in his throat, blocking his air passage.

"I asked her why she was breaking your heart and hers—"

"Hers?"

"Aw, hell yeah, man. She smiles a good game, says all the right words, but she's in deep pain. It's etched in the pinched lines around her eyes, and the dull gaze that used to be a lot brighter."

God, he'd loved her bright eyes, so green and vibrant.

"Anyhow, she ignored my questions, but asked me some."

His chin lifted. "What did she ask?"

"Only two, Jace. And they were very specific, and very telling."

"Okay. What?"

"If you'd left the guard, and if you'd signed on with DWB."

He blinked, then sucked in a breath as everything became so damn clear it gleamed. "I'm such a fucking idiot."

His buddy's snicker received an answering snigger from Beckham. "I wouldn't say that exactly. You are an idiot at times, but…"

"Thanks." He laughed for the first time in weeks.

"You're welcome. And I happen to know Holly's going to be at The Pub in an hour for a farewell dinner."

He smiled and held out his hand as he strode forward. "Thanks again, Tanner."

"Anytime, man," he said, slapping his shoulder before drawing back. "So, what are you going to do?"

"Talk some sense into my stubborn girlfriend."

"That's the spirit. Go get her." Then his grin turned into a grimace. "But you might want to think about taking a shower first to wash the horse off you."

Chapter Eighteen

Holly made it through dinner with only a few tears, mostly shed by Shayla and Kerri complaining about their hormones.

"I can't believe you're not going to be here to see my baby," Shayla said, pulling in for her third hug.

"Or mine." Kerri sniffled.

"I already told you, I'll be driving back down for a long weekend in four weeks. You two should've popped by then."

The expectant mothers nodded.

"This little one better be on time. I'm kind of done carrying her, and can do without the swollen ankles."

"Yeah, what ankles? I have cankles." Sticking out her foot, Kerri glanced down beyond her belly and grimaced. "I can't even get regular shoes on. Have to wear slip-ons a size bigger than normal.

"I love your cankles," Connor said, limping up to his wife to plant a kiss on her cheek. "You're so damn beautiful."

This got *awwws* from Shayla and Caitlin, while Holly's heart seized, wishing…

She blew out a breath and lifted her chin. *Not prudent to waste time on a false hope. Or dream.* Her father's words echoed in her head, and this time, she was taking his advice willingly.

"To Holly." Jordan lifted her glass, and suddenly everyone had a glass of some kind of drink in the air. "May you find your own happiness."

She feared that emotion was going to be elusive for a long time, but she smiled, putting her best effort into it, too.

"To Holly…"

Her heart dipped to her knees at the sound of the familiar, deep voice of the man she loved.

Jace appeared out of nowhere, striding straight for her with a glass in his hand, and his heart in his eyes. "May she find her happiness with me."

"Here, here," everyone echoed, then cheered.

She didn't lift her glass. She just stared, trying to decipher his meaning.

Tanner came up behind him and smiled at her. "You should really toast that one, Hol."

She knew something was going on, but for the life of her, her mind couldn't grasp it.

"You're leaving," she managed to say, setting her glass on the table because her hands were shaking so bad.

"Yeah, in about two weeks. You saw to that."

She reeled back, wondering how the hell he knew. She hadn't told a soul. And judging by the smile spreading across his face, erasing every single last doubt and scrap of sadness from his eyes, she had the sinking feeling it was her who just told him without meaning to.

Dammit.

"It's true." He stepped close and reached out to grasp her shoulders when she made to move away. "You took that job because you were afraid I wasn't going to go."

"Were you?"

He shrugged. "I don't rightfully know, Holly. And I guess we never will because you decided to play God and take that choice away from me."

"Take away? Jace, you were going to throw away your dream. On me. No way in hell was I going to stand by and let you." She reached up to cup his face. "You are a great doctor. The world needs you. I could never live with myself if I took you from your plans, and all those sick people you're about to help."

"And what about you, Hol?"

"What about me?" she hiccupped. *Dammit.*

"Do you need me?"

God...more than air.

But she couldn't tell him that. No. He needed to go. She needed to get out of there. She needed to stop the damn tears from spilling down her face, betraying every secret she was trying to hide.

With a rough groan, he pulled her in close and held her tight. "Damn it, Holly. I love you, and I need you. Very much. Much more than I need to help others. Yeah, that was my life's goal." He drew back and cupped her face. "But, don't you see? That all changed when you came to town. You are what makes me a better man. You ground me. *You* are the center of my universe."

She was shaking, and said to hell with the tears. "I love you, too, Jace, so much." She burrowed into him, holding him tight, soaking in his calming presence, his strength, letting him heal the heart she'd mistakenly thought it had made sense to break.

"I know. So much so you were willing to sacrifice your happiness for mine."

Nodding, she drew back and stared up at him. "Yes. I know in my heart you were meant to join DWB. I'm glad you did. And am *so* proud."

"The thing is, you make me happy, so...I have a proposition for you, Miss Let-me-put-you-first-and-not-think-about-me."

She gave a watery laugh and waited for him to continue. "Okay…"

"Come with me."

The whole room sucked in a collective breath.

"What?"

"Come with me. You can join, too. You don't have to be a doctor to help out."

Her heart shifted, lifting slightly in her chest. Could she? She no longer supported her mom or brother. She only had herself to worry about now.

"And bring your camera. Come document the places we go and the people we see. I've no doubt you can create something the public will treasure as much as we will."

Tears streamed down her face now, and that of several of their friends. Not all of them female. Connor brushed his face a few times.

"What do you say?"

She sucked in a breath and nodded. "Yes."

Jace let out a whoop just before he lifted her off the ground and spun them around, kind of mimicking her heart at that very moment.

"Why didn't I think of that?" she asked as he set her feet back down. "You're so smart."

"Hello…Doctor here." He waved at her.

She punched his arm. "Goof."

"Yeah, a goof who loves you, and does *not* want to be away from you ever again. Promise me you'll never put my needs before yours?"

She laughed and shook her head. "Yeah, as soon as you put yours before mine."

His smile was bright enough to light the room. "I think we make a perfect pair. You know how much I love you, right?"

"As much as I love you."

He pulled her in tight and buried his face in her hair, inhaling deeply. “Exactly.”

Jace drew back to cup Holly’s face and very purposely lowered his head to kiss her, sending a wild cheer through their family and friends.

Epilogue

Two weeks later…

At their real going away party, Holly was smiling and leaning into Jace, excited and content at the prospect of flying away with him in the morning. Because she'd already had a passport, there hadn't been much red tape to attach her to his contingent with DWB.

"Happy?" he asked, nuzzling her ear.

"Mmm…very," she replied, turning slightly to slide her hands up his chest. "You?"

"Could be better."

"Better?" She pulled back to stare up at him. "How?"

"You could be naked and writhing beneath me," he replied, going back to cause more damage to her pulse with a hot trail of kisses down her neck.

"Get a room," Tanner said, coming up behind them.

Jace drew back and smiled. "Maybe you should."

"Yeah." She nodded. "What's with the looks you keep exchanging with…*Gwen*, is it? Brandi's friend that came back with her from Pennsylvania to fill in for Kerri when she has her baby." Which would hopefully be this week, since the poor thing was already six days overdue.

The two weeks since Jace had propositioned Holly had been hectic. For everyone. Especially Shayla and Kevin.

Sarah Kay Dalton arrived two weeks early, on the day after Holly's first going away party. The sweet little girl was named after both grandmothers, and the pride and joy of her parents, and her big sister. Amelia even sported the T-shirt claiming she was happy to be a big sister. Her friend said her oldest daughter wouldn't take it off, so Kevin, of course, went out and bought her ten more.

"How's Brandi?" Tanner asked, changing the subject, one that brought concern to all of them.

"Not great," she replied, her gaze drifting to the pale woman, smiling and chatting, but all with a shadow of pain in her eyes.

Cole had lent the designer and her husband his jet to rush up to Pennsylvania a few days ago to attend the funeral of a fallen soldier, who happened to be her youngest brother's best friend. "She's really concerned for Keiffer. He's the one who found the body."

She couldn't even imagine what the poor guy, the whole community was going through, dealing with the young man's suicide.

"It's not going to be easy," Jace said. "And Keiffer is going to need help, but won't want it."

She nodded, knowing he was talking from experience.

"Speaking of help. Let's get back to you, Tanner," she said, figuring it was best to change the subject. "Gwen's gorgeous. A former supermodel I believe?"

"And blonde," Jace added, both of them knowing their friend's penchant for blondes. "And if memory serves me correctly, you two kind of disappeared at Brandi's wedding reception last September."

She snapped her gaze to the frowning cowboy. "Really?" Holly snuggled into Jace. "Oh, I'm almost sorry we're leaving tomorrow, Jace. Something tells me things are about to heat up in Harland County."

♥

Sparks reignite when one-nighers reunite. Can the firefighter/Guardsman convince the reforming bad girl she's worth fighting for, or will she leave before he finds the courage to volunteer his heart?

♥

Her Volunteer Cowboy

Harland County Series: Book Six/Tanner

Coming August 4, 2015

In the 12 Alarm Cowboy boxed set,

then released on its own in September!

♥

Phoebe's temporary gig as a substitute music teacher at an elementary school is just what the burnt out, former Broadway star needs to regroup from a demanding, and lately, unsatisfying career. Exposing children to the magic of music has reawakened her love for the basics. The Poconos is a great place to find herself, and she was finding her frequent encounters with the handsome, single father of one of her students has reawakened a different type of passion.

But he's made it clear he's not looking for permanent, and for the first time in her life, she's not looking for temporary. Maybe what his locked up, guarded heart needs is a little song.

♥

Wyne and Song

Citizen Soldier Series: Book Three/Ethan

Coming November 2015

♥

***

For announcements about upcoming releases and exclusive contests:
Join Donna's Newsletter
Visit me at: www.donnamichaelsauthor.com
***

Harland County Series

Visit my **Harland County Series Page** at my website www.donnamichaelsauthor.com for release information and updates!

Prequel Book .05: Harland County Christmas-Novella
Book One: Her Fated Cowboy
Book Two: Her Unbridled Cowboy
Book Three: Her Uniform Cowboy
Book Four: Her Forever Cowboy
Book Five Her Healing Cowboy

Coming soon:
Book Six: Her Volunteer Cowboy-Novella (12 Pack-Alarm boxed set)

Become a *Cowboy Tamer!*

Drop me a line at donna_michaels@msn.com and request some Cowboy-Tamer swag!

***

Harland County Series

Prequel Book .05: *Harland County Christmas*

NOR Reviewer Top Pick – Night Owl Reviews

Accounting major Jen has one more year before she graduates and moves out of Harland County to find a corporate job and maybe a good-looking businessman to boot. Cowboys were handsome and fun, but they didn't stick. Neither did ranch hands. Experience has taught her they come and go, and some took a piece of her heart with them. Well, no more handsome, sexy, cowboys. She wanted a stay around, stable, lifetime type of guy.

Then she returns to the family ranch for the summer to discover Brock, the hot, one-night stand she'd given herself permission to enjoy right after finals, is the new ranch hand. And dang it, she's just as drawn to his sexy grin, gorgeous green eyes and quiet strength. As the summer ends, classes resume, and the holidays near, the handsome, alpha cowboy has her rethinking her future. So does the unborn baby she's carrying. Maybe sticking around Harland County isn't so bad—if she could get Brock to stay, and break out of the 'leave Jen and move on to another ranch' mold.

***

Harland County Series

Book One: *Her Fated Cowboy*

NOR Reviewer Top Pick – Night Owl Reviews

L.A. cop Jordan Masters Ryan has a problem. Her normal method of meeting a crisis head-on and taking it down won't work. Not this time. Not when fate is her adversary. Having kept her from the man she thought she'd always marry, the same fickle fate took away the man she eventually did. Thrown back into the path of her first love, she finds hers is not the only heart fate has damaged.

Widower and software CEO, Cole McCall fills his days with computer codes and his free time working the family's cattle ranch. Blaming himself for his wife's death, he's become hard and bitter. When his visiting former neighbor sets out to delete the firewall around his heart, he discovers there's no protection against the Jordan virus. Though she understands his pain and reawakens his soul, will it be enough for Cole to overcome his past and embrace their fated hearts?

***

Harland County Series

Book Two: *Her Unbridled Cowboy*

NOR Reviewer Top Pick – Night Owl Reviews

Homeless and unemployed thanks to an earthquake, divorced California chef Kerri Masters agrees to head back to her hometown to help plan her sister's Texas wedding. It must be her weakened state that has her eyeing the neighbor she used to follow around as a child. Her tastes tend towards gentlemen in suits, cultured, and neatly groomed— not a dimple-glaring, giant of a cowboy. He's big and virile, and makes her want things the inadequacies brought out during her divorce keep her from carrying out.

Connor McCall's brotherly feelings for the pesky former neighbor disappear when the grown up version steps on his ranch in her fancy clothes and shiny heels. Too bad she's a city girl, because he has no use for them. Three times he tried to marry one, and three times the engagements failed. He's not looking for number four no matter how much his body is all for jumping back in the saddle and showing the sexy chef just how it feels to be loved by a cowboy.

Turns out the earthquake was nothing compared to the passionate, force of nature of an unbridled cowboy, and Kerri learns far more about herself, and Connor, than she ever expected. But when events put his trust in her on the line, will he choose his heart or his pride?

Harland County Series

Book Three: *Her Uniform Cowboy*

Crowned Heart of Excellence – InD'tale Magazine
****Voted BEST COWBOY in a Book/Readers' Choice-LRC****
****Finalist in BTS eMag Red Capet Book Awards for Best Romance & Best Book****
****NOR Reviewer Top Pick – Night Owl Reviews****

Desperate for change after a verbally abusive relationship, Brandi Wyne leaves a symphony career, her family, and the Poconos to fall back on a designing degree and a chance to renovate a restaurant/pub in Texas. Even though part of a National Guard family, she'd sworn off military men when the last one proved less than supportive of her thyroid condition and subsequent weight gain. Too bad her body seems to forget that fact whenever she's near the very hot, very military local sheriff.

Texas Army National Guard First Sergeant Kade Dalton never planned on becoming Harland County Sheriff or the attraction to a curvy, military-hating designer from Pennsylvania. Heavy with guilt from the death of a soldier under his command during a recent deployment, and dealing with his co-owned horse ranch and a bungling young deputy, it's hard most days just to keep his sanity. But it's the Yankee bombshell who threatens not only his sanity, but tempts his body...and his heart.

Fighting their attraction becomes a losing battle, and Kade soon finds sanctuary in the arms of the beautiful designer. Does he really have the right to saddle Brandi with his stress issues? And if so, can he take a chance on the town's newest resident not abandoning him like others in his past?

Harland County Series

Book Four: *Her Forever Cowboy*

NOR Reviewer Top Pick – Night Owl Reviews
Crowned Heart of Excellence – InD'tale Magazine
RONE Award Nominee-InD'tale Magazine
****July's Read of the Month/Readers' Choice-SSLY Blog****
****Top Ten finisher for Best Romance at P&E****
****BTS eMagazine Red Carpet Book Awards Nominee****

Single mother, Shayla Ryan, longs to put down roots to create a stable environment for her baby girl and her younger sister, but the threat of her abusive, ex-con father finding them has made that almost impossible. Her newest residence in Harland County, however, holds a lot of appeal, especially in the form of a Casanova cowboy with eye-catching good looks and easy charm. Those two qualities took her down the wrong road before, and though the sexy cowboy interferes with her pulse, she can't let her heart get in the way of the safety of her family, or give it to someone who doesn't believe in forever.

If there's one thing software company vice president, Kevin Dalton, loves more than puzzles, it's women. Size, shape, race doesn't matter as long as they don't want a relationship—he's not looking to repeat the past, and more than happy to remain single. Until two beautiful redheads drop him to his knees—one with her cutie-pie smile, the other with her elbow. Too bad the elbow-toting beauty is both hot and puzzling. A killer combination too strong to resist. And without realizing it, the redheads slowly rewrite the code around his heart.

But when the danger from Shayla's past shows up, can he rise to the challenge to keep them safe...and really be what they need? A *forever* cowboy?

***

Citizen Soldier Series

Book One: *Wyne and Dine*

NOR Reviewer Top Pick – Night Owl Reviews

Lea Gablonski has two dreams: To work at a museum in NYC, and to gain other-than-sisterly attention from her best friend's brother. So far, she's 0 for 0. Though her MA in History is just a wall decoration at her family's diner where she's working while her dad recovers from surgery, she enjoys her visual encounters with the sexiest man alive—even though he would sooner pat her on the head than take her to bed.

Military born and bred, Battalion Supply Sergeant Benjamin Wyne thrives on order and control in his fulltime career in the PA National Guard, and in his personal life. But when he's forced to ask his childhood sweetheart's younger sister to pose as his girlfriend to thwart unwanted advances from his boss' wife, his world turns chaotic. Lea is sweet and hot and tastes so damn good he's addicted. When the attraction takes on a new level at his sister's wedding, his carefully guarded heart begins to thaw.

But he's seen many relationships go south. If he takes a chance and gives up control, will Lea be like her sister and leave him for a career in the big city? Yet, if he doesn't, will the best damn thing to ever enter his life become history?

***

Time-shift Heroes Series

Book One: Captive Hero

****2012 RONE Awards Nominee Best Time Travel****

When Marine Corps test pilot, Captain Samantha Sheppard accidentally flies back in time and inadvertently saves the life of a WWII VMF Black Sheep pilot, she changes history and makes a crack decision to abduct him back to the present. With the timeline in jeopardy, she hides the handsome pilot at her secluded cabin in the Colorado wilderness.

But convincing her sexy, stubborn captive that he is now in another century proves harder than she anticipated—and soon it becomes difficult to tell who is captor and who is captive when the more he learns about the future, the more Sam discovers about the past, and the soul-deep connection between them.

As their flames of desire burn into overdrive, her flying Ace makes a historical discovery that threatens her family's very existence. Sam's fears are taken to new heights when she realizes the only way to fix the time-line is to sacrifice her captive hero...or is it?
Can love truly survive the test of time?

Time-shift Heroes Series

Visit my **Time-shift Heroes Series Page** for release information and updates!

Book One: Captive Hero
Book Two: Future Hero
Book Three: Unintended Hero

***

Cowboy-Fiancé

Honky Tonk Hearts Series with
The Wild Rose Press
by Donna Michaels

****4 Star RT Magazine Review*&*NOR Reviewer Top Pick****
****Going Global! Now being translated into Japanese as a MANGA!****

Finn Brennan was used to his brother playing practical jokes, but this time he'd gone too far--sending him a *woman* as a ranch hand, and not just a woman, but a Marine.

When Lt. Camilla Walker's CO asks her to help out at his family's dude ranch until he returns from deployment, she never expected to be thrust into a mistaken engagement to his sexy, cowboy twin--a former Navy SEAL who *hates* the Corps.

The Corps took Finn's father, his girlfriend and threatened his naval career. He's worked hard for another shot at getting back to active duty and won't let his brother's prank interfere. The last thing he needs is the temptation of a headstrong, unyielding, hot Marine getting in the way.

COWBOY PAYBACK
(Brett's story)
Coming Soon!
through The Wild Rose Press

***

<u>She Does Know Jack</u>
A Romantic Comedy Suspense
by <u>Donna Michaels</u>

****NOR Reviewer Top Pick****

Former Army Ranger Capt. Jack 'Dodger' Anderson would rather run naked through a minefield in the Afghan desert than participate in a reality television show, but when his brother Matthew begins to receive threats, Jack quickly becomes Matthew's shadow. As if the investigation isn't baffling enough, he has to contend with the addition of a beautiful and vaguely familiar new contestant.

Security specialist, Brielle Chapman reluctantly agrees to help her uncle by going undercover as a contestant on the *Meet Your Mate* reality show. Having nearly failed on a similar assignment, she wants to prove she still has a future in this business. But when the brother of the *groom* turns out to be Dodger, the only one-nighter she ever had—while in disguise from a prior undercover case—her job becomes harder. Does he recognize her? And how can she investigate with their sizzling attraction fogging her brain? Determined to finish the job, she brings the case to a surprising climax, uncovers the culprit and *meets* her own *mate*.

***

Thanks for reading!